Her childhood love has returned. How will she marry his brother now?

"Ellie, come away with me. We'll be married in Vicksburg by morning."

Eleanor yanked her hand from his touch, though it took all her strength. "You said you came home to be forgiven. Do you think anyone would offer forgiveness if you stole your brother's betrothed?" She looked deep into the hazel eyes, and she saw remorse there for his words. Eleanor reached out and touched his cheek. "I know you want to please your father, and the way to do that is to let things be. Andrew and I shall be happy. . .

KRISTIN BILLERBECK lives in the Silicon Valley with her husband, Bryed, and their four young children, Trey, Jonah, Seth, and Ellena. Kristin enjoys reading, painting, and assisting her husband in teaching Sunday school. Visit Kristin on the web at www.kristinbillerbeck.com.

HEARTSONG PRESENTS

The Prodigal's Welcome

Kristin Billerbeck

Heartsong Presents

To Beth, my best friend since I was four. Little did our parents know what trouble they would cause putting us together in that catechism class. With all my love, Kristin

A note from the author:
I love to hear from my readers! You may correspond with me by writing: **Kristin Billerbeck**
Author Relations
PO Box 719
Uhrichsville, OH 44683

ISBN 1-58660-377-9

THE PRODIGAL'S WELCOME

All Scripture quotations, unless otherwise noted, are taken from the King James Version of the Bible.

All of the characters and events in this book are fictitious. Any resemblance to actual persons, living or dead, or to actual events is purely coincidental.

Cover design by Robyn Martins.

PRINTED IN THE U.S.A.

one

"You've come back." Eleanor blinked back tears but couldn't rein in the emotion that caused her to tremble. The ghost of her past stood before her, as real as any Confederate soldier.

"California was not the land of riches I thought it would be." Nathaniel's sheepish grin confirmed her worst fears. He had squandered everything.

"Things are not as you left them, but I'm sure you've realized that would be the case with the war."

Eleanor hadn't meant to sound cold, but how could Nathaniel expect to pick up where he'd left off? Except for his more manly frame from hard labor, he looked the same. The familiar hazel eyes with flecks of gold stared at her; the warm smile, the knowing look all took her back six years when she had loved this man with her heart and soul.

"My father has welcomed me home, Eleanor. With his blessings."

Eleanor awoke from her memories. Did he expect her to do the same? "I'm sure your brother has other thoughts on the matter. Did you know Andrew became a captain in the war?" She waited for his reaction and watched him flinch. "Did you know he lost an arm?" *Oh, Nathaniel, did you know he asked me to marry him?*

Nathaniel's gaze dropped to the rich earth. "I did."

"I hope your dreams were realized in California, Nathaniel." *For ours died a long time ago, when Yankees invaded.* Eleanor picked up her skirt and walked toward Rosamond, her

5

once-stately home. The sight of it forced her to face him again. "Your brother, and men like him, are the reason our homes are standing today." Her firm stance meant nothing against his apologetic gaze.

"Eleanor, please. I was a fool." He touched her shoulder, and she shivered at his touch. Turning to look into his eyes, she felt her heart throbbing under his gaze. Unwittingly, she fell into his open arms, and her body racked with tears at the comfort she found in his embrace. Without thought, she drew closer to his chest.

"I am so glad you've come home, Nathaniel. I'm glad you are safe." His familiar scent filled all of her senses, reminding her of what was, what might have been. No matter what her head told her, her heart still loved this man, still ached to have him near her. But his being home was enough. It would have to be.

"I've come home to stay. I'm done with foolishness."

"Are you, Nathaniel?" She forced herself away, straightening her gown. "But I'll not hold it against you, Nathaniel. Welcome home. I pray you'll make the most of your new life."

Eleanor tilted her chin, summoned her remaining shreds of courage, and turned. If it weren't for the war, she might have stayed in his arms forever—forgiving him and his childish ways—but she was stronger now. She had changed since the war. Everyone had. Everyone except Nathaniel, who remained unscathed by battles and Yankees.

"Eleanor, will you have me?" He opened his hands, willing her to come back to him. "I know I do not deserve you."

Eleanor's breath abandoned her, and she fought the urge to run to him. "You don't know?" she whispered.

"I know you are angry. You have every right, but I've changed, Eleanor. I'm not the boy who left—"

She interrupted him. "I'm engaged to your brother, Nathaniel. I thought your father would have told you." She softened at his wounded expression, and, for once, she felt like the traitor.

"Eleanor." The hollow sound of her name sent a sickening swirl through her stomach. "My brother? Andrew?"

"Your brother has been here, Nathaniel." She needed to justify herself. How dare he look at her as if she had been to blame? "He fought for me, and my family's home, our heritage. While you ran to seek your fortune in the wilderness, Andrew was steadfast and true. The war has been hard on everyone. I need something to hold firm, to be solid; and that is Andrew." Eleanor stood a little straighter.

"Slaves were not your heritage, Eleanor. You always told me you would fight to see them free. You've been listening to your father for too long."

"Who else was I to listen to, Nathaniel? The idealistic man I thought shared my visions left, without so much as a handshake."

The accusations were flowing freely now. "You were *my* fiancée! You would marry my own brother?" Nathaniel's voice carried so the house servants looked on with interest.

"Keep your voice down. We needn't share our business with everyone." Eleanor waved the attention off and focused on Nathaniel again, clenching her teeth in annoyance. "I assumed our engagement was nullified when you left me a note telling me of your future in California. Why ever would you expect me to be free six years later? Do you find me that unpalatable?"

"Of course not, but I didn't expect you to marry my brother either."

Nathaniel crossed his arms, as though he had a right to be upset. Irritation plunged through Eleanor's veins.

"In case you haven't noticed, there's a shortage of marriageable men since the war, but even if there weren't I would be engaged to your brother. He has proven himself to be a hero, and so much more."

"But do you love him?"

Eleanor gulped noticeably. "Of course I love him."

Nathaniel stepped closer, and she felt his proximity to her feet. She curled her toes in her boots, needing to let off her restless energy. His familiar scent felt too intimate.

"Ellie," he whispered.

"Don't call me that. You have no right to call me that. Think of your brother, Nathaniel," she begged him. "Think of me." She pressed a hand to her chest.

Nathaniel retreated, and she breathed an audible sigh of relief.

"It's not over, Ellie. I came back for you, and I'll make my brother understand. I'll make you understand. God has changed my heart. He has redeemed me from the pit, and I want to share it with you. I want to—"

"It doesn't always matter what one wants, Nathaniel. Think of your brother. Think of all he has been through, all he has endured while you spent your inheritance on what suited your whims and squandered your heritage. The Nathaniel I loved would never have knowingly hurt his family."

The descending sun caught the gold flecks in his eyes, and Eleanor was transported to another time and place. The horses whinnied in the background, while Nathaniel held her hand in the green, spring grass. He had looked at her with a man's eyes then, and she remembered how the sun had caught the gold that afternoon as well.

"God has granted me forgiveness, Ellie. Won't you?"

Eleanor was startled from the images of a happier, carefree time. "I forgive you, Nathaniel, but I will still marry your brother in one month. You should wish us every happiness. It is the least you can do."

"Miss Eleanor! Miss Eleanor, your father is asking for you." The shrill voice of Mrs. Patterson, their family housekeeper, called her.

"I must go, Nathaniel. Take care of yourself." Eleanor turned toward her great house, now scorched with remnants of the war and badly in need of whitewash. She willed herself not to turn back and nearly choked on the tears she held at bay. By combining her plantation with Andrew's, she hoped to keep them both alive with the freed slaves who remained. The workers were indeed few. Everything seemed so easy minutes ago, but Nathaniel's return had changed everything.

❧

Nathaniel ambled back toward Woodacre, his family plantation. "I should have known." He shook his head in anger, his teeth still clenched. His brother's triumphant smile at Nathaniel's return suddenly made sense. Andrew's admiration of Ellie had never been a secret. He had always been jealous over the connection Nathaniel and she shared. And now Andrew had managed to end the special bond, once and for all. Nathaniel chastised himself. He had no one to blame but himself.

"Where have you been, little brother?" Andrew's victorious tone caught Nathaniel's attention. "As if I didn't know. You've been to see my fiancée? I could have saved you the trip, dear brother." Andrew smirked.

He still wore his Confederate uniform, his left armhole stitched closed to hide the war wound. Nathaniel felt Andrew's entire appearance was merely a costume meant to taunt him for his past sins, as if he were saying, *Here I am—the righteous brother, the one who did as he was told and earned Father's favor.*

"Why did you keep your engagement a secret?" Nathaniel watched his brother's smile disappear. "I should think you'd announce it to the world. This is quite a victory for you. You'll own Rosamond, too, I suppose."

"I thought it best you hear it from Ellie. I feared you might not believe me. I can see by your face you believe it now. Ellie deserves to be cared for."

The use of her childhood nickname sent chills through Nathaniel's spine. No one but he and her mother had ever called her that until now.

"There are so many women, Andrew. Why Ellie?" Nathaniel couldn't keep the anguish from his voice.

"*Eleanor* has wasted six years of her life, Nathaniel. She's been pining for you, swearing you'd return to her. But I knew differently. I knew you'd come back destitute and probably married with a few children, as well. You surprised me there. She finally agreed to marry a man who truly loves her, not just with words, but in action. Something you've failed to do, dear brother." Andrew patted Nathaniel's shoulder.

There was a bit of warmth in the act, and Nathaniel reminded himself it was he who had left. Wouldn't he want Ellie to be happy? Wouldn't he have wanted her to be a mother and share in all that life had to offer her? He was still so selfish. His conversion hadn't changed his desires.

"Will you love her, Andrew? Or just the land she can bring you?"

"I shall not dignify that with an answer."

Nathaniel lowered himself to the rich earth under his feet. Every part of his will had disappeared. Six years in California, and he had come home with nothing. Not the wealth he'd promised himself or the new faith he'd claimed. Or so it seemed. He thought loving this Jesus, this new God, who was more than a weekly visit in the family pew, would change everything, but it hadn't appeared to change anything.

I'll prove my worth, Lord. You did not redeem me for nothing, and I'll show them all out of love for You. I ask for nothing. Nothing, but the chance to be on Woodacre again and see that my brother cares for Ellie. My precious Ellie.

❧

"Eleanor, who was that you were speaking with?" Mrs. Patterson lowered a brow. "It's not proper for young ladies to be conversing with a gentleman alone. Especially an engaged woman."

Eleanor laughed. "Mrs. Patterson, after the war there's hardly anything that isn't proper anymore. Just this afternoon I spent overseeing the tilling of the soil. That's hardly worthy of any belle."

"Well, you shouldn't be out there anyway. You know how your father feels on such matters."

"I also know his overseer wouldn't dare lay a hand on the men when I'm around. So I stay close by. The Bible says we are to submit to those in authority, and President Andrew Johnson is our president. I submit, but that scoundrel taking the overseer's place doesn't seem to."

"Johnson is no president of mine, the traitor."

"The Bible says—"

"Do not try to dissuade my thoughts, Eleanor. You're still your father's daughter, and you're not a married woman yet. Here on Rosamond we still keep up appearances, no matter what the Yankees tried to do to us. If we give up our discretion, why, we're no better than the likes of them."

"Yes, Ma'am."

"Now who was that man you were speaking with?"

"Nathaniel Pemberton, Ma'am. He has returned from California."

Mrs. Patterson mumbled something Ellie was surely better off not hearing, but she spoke the end of her thoughts clearly. "You stay away from that fitful coward, Eleanor. He's not worthy to walk on Rosamond soil."

"His father has forgiven him. He's been welcomed home with open arms."

The older woman pursed her lips. "Well, he's not welcome here. What Mr. Pemberton feels led to do is between him and the Almighty, but as far as I'm concerned, Nathaniel Pemberton isn't worth the rags I saw on his back."

"In case you've forgotten, he's to be my brother in a month's time. I suggest you forgive him for all our sakes. If our plantations are to thrive, we've got to work together in our new situation. The war hasn't helped any of us."

"Nathaniel did his family more harm than the Union gunboats did to our fair city. Your father will not take kindly to Mr. Pemberton's welcoming back such a turncoat. I can tell you he will not be invited to the nuptials."

Eleanor sighed. She knew what her father would have to say about Nathaniel's return, and it probably wasn't fit for a lady's ears. But she had already forgiven Nathaniel. She couldn't help herself. Nathaniel didn't have a cruel bone in his body. He'd been misguided and wistful about his once-future plans, but who could blame a man for following his dream? It would have been different if he'd come back a wealthy man, successful in his pursuits. All would have been forgiven, but Nathaniel was being punished for his failure. Of that, she had no doubt.

"You needn't worry about him. He'll be Under-the-Hill soon enough." Mrs. Patterson said, referring to the town's seedier part of town. "Coward," she added.

Cowardice had nothing to do with Nathaniel Pemberton. If anything, cowardice had personified the town of Natchez. If it hadn't fallen so early, none of the many buildings would be standing. As it was, Natchez wasn't much worse for the wear, except for the slave situation, a few gunboat marks, and the looting. The money and privilege the town enjoyed were far more important to its inhabitants than fighting a war. They planned to run their town their way regardless of the outcome of any violence.

"Eleanor." Her father's gruff voice halted her thoughts.

"Yes, Father."

"I've had word from Woodacre that Nathaniel has returned." Her father's darkened brow said it all. He was worried she'd run away with the man she once loved.

"Yes, Sir." Eleanor tried to act unaffected.

"You'll not speak with him. The Lord only knows what terrible ideas he's brought from that forsaken California. Not to mention the diseases known to be out West."

"Father, Nathaniel doesn't mean any harm. He—" He coughed abruptly, and Eleanor corrected herself. "Master Pemberton."

"Eleanor, I know your mother fancied Master Pemberton for you at one time, but that all changed when he showed himself to be a milksop. His brother is far better suited to you, and I'm only sorry we didn't see it earlier."

"Father, Nathaniel—Master Pemberton—couldn't have known there was to be a war. He went before—"

"Everyone knew there was to be a war, Eleanor!" her father bellowed. "When the government tried to exert its will on the states, it was only a matter of time. South Carolina did what we all had to do, and Nathaniel had to see the fire coming. It's probably why he left so quickly."

"Reconstruction has begun, Father. We must move forward." Why was she defending Nathaniel? Hadn't she said the same things to him? But, somehow, hearing someone else speak of her beloved that way was far more difficult than she'd have imagined. She chastised herself for thinking of him as her beloved. Andrew was her beloved. *No, Lord, he is my fiancé, and there is such a chasm between the two. Help me think properly of Andrew, Lord. Please.*

"I don't care what *their* law says—no one's going to tell me how to run my plantation. We'll set up black codes as all our neighbors have."

Eleanor cringed. Black codes were plantation speak for the continuation of slavery. They would make former slaves sign away their rights for the *privilege* of working, with severe punishments for anyone who dared not complete a contract.

"Father, the Negroes just want food and shelter. They're not asking for a lot, but you've got to care for them properly. They're people. The Bible says there was neither slave nor free-man in Christ. The men are not getting enough to eat, Father, and they're having to steal from each other to get enough food for the day's work."

"If they don't like it, they can leave." He looked to the ground. "Until the codes are official, of course."

Eleanor thinned her eyes. "It's a new day, Father. You've got to learn to adapt, or the Yankees will be back. We must find a new way of running Rosamond. The way Mother ran it. Lincoln said the Union must reunite for charity's sake."

"And Lincoln is dead for charity's sake."

Eleanor decided it best to drop the subject. Seeing the pain the war had caused, all its death and destruction, it was no wonder her father felt as he did. Although Natchez had been spared the worst kind of ruin, the town had still lost many of its sons. No one could forget that. It was impossible to think of Yankees without thinking of loss.

"Andrew is coming for dinner tonight, Eleanor. You shall not let your beau down. You look as if you've been in the fields all day."

Eleanor smiled nervously. There was a reason she looked that way. "Yes, Father."

She excused herself to go to the house and climbed the familiar stairs, but she stopped on the landing, gazing into an old portrait. Her mother looked back, and Eleanor choked back tears at the sight of her. "You would forgive him, Mother. I know you would." She let her eyes close in reverie. *Oh, Lord, give me the strength to marry Andrew.*

two

Dinner proved to be an odd little affair, and Eleanor tapped her feet incessantly to endure the drawn-out evening. Nathaniel was there in spirit, though unwelcome by all, his invisible presence interrupting Eleanor's every attempt at conversation. She could think of no one else.

"Ellie," Andrew said.

He'd taken to calling her Ellie when Nathaniel returned, and Eleanor didn't like it one bit. It was a childish name, not worthy of a woman who would soon be mistress of Woodacre, and it only called attention to the closeness she and Nathaniel once shared.

"I hear the ladies are organizing a quilting circle again. Will you be a part of it?"

Eleanor pushed the food about on her plate. "I shouldn't think so, Andrew. I'll have much to do preparing the rooms after our wedding."

"It's been a time since Mother was there to add a lady's touch. Father and—" He halted, clearly stumbling over the name of Nathaniel. "Father and his sons are looking forward to having the niceties of life brought back to Woodacre. I daresay the housekeeper has been driven to insanity seeing to us. You may dismiss her if need be."

"That shan't be necessary, I'm sure." Eleanor forced a smile.

An eternity of idle, pointless conversation followed before the men retired to the study. Eleanor promptly excused herself and flew down the back steps, stopping outside the kitchen house. She gasped for breath, grateful for the cold air rather than the stagnant feel of the dining room. She sniffed the crisp air, thankful for the smell of fall leaves in the night breeze.

"Ellie," his voice came to her in a whisper, and for a moment she thought she dreamed it. But Nathaniel stepped from the shadows, and her heart pounded faster. "Do you remember how we'd meet here when we were younger?" His tall frame sent her mind soaring, and she recalled the way his hazel eyes caused flutters in her stomach. Just as it felt now. *Nathaniel has grown into a stunningly handsome man,* she admitted to herself. "Do you remember, Ellie? We'd wait until the men retired, when we were supposed to be tucked away for the night, and we'd come here to the kitchen and play jacks."

She turned away to avoid his warm gaze in the moonlight. "You shouldn't be here. Father would have your head if he knew you were bothering me."

"Am I bothering you?" The self-assuredness in his voice hadn't changed a bit. Nathaniel understood his power over her, and it was all the more reason to squelch it now.

"Of course, you're bothering me. If you hadn't noticed, I was having a fine dinner party with my fiancé. A dinner party which you were not invited to, or didn't you notice?"

Nathaniel clicked his tongue. "When has your father ever willingly invited me? I'm going to prove myself, Ellie. I may not be any type of Confederate hero; but I was wrong, and I intend to make up for it."

"I shall be the first to congratulate you when you do. If you'll excuse me."

Eleanor hiked up her skirt and turned to leave, but Nathaniel grasped her shoulders, stopping her.

"Eleanor, I know you believe in me. I know you understand I didn't know a thing about the war."

"You knew *when* it was happening. Don't tell me you didn't

know your country was in a war. California is not that far away. Many men returned from the West to fight, and even Europe, but you didn't, Nathaniel."

"I wasn't saved, Ellie. Would you rather I'd died in battle than meet you for all eternity? God had His plan. My selfishness was great, but He has used it to bring me back to Him."

"Nathaniel, do you expect me to believe that God ordained your flight?"

"No, that's not what I meant. I just meant if I had died in the war, I would not meet you in heaven."

"Don't be ridiculous. You've been attending church since you were a boy. What is this talk of not being saved before?"

"I've been fidgeting in the pew since I was a boy. I never knew eternal life rested in Him. Not until a spicy old prospector told me the gospel, and I grasped it in my heart by confessing my sins."

Eleanor looked into his eyes and knew he spoke the truth. Nathaniel wasn't the dramatic type, especially not about religious conversation. If he said he'd found grace, he had.

All at once a fearful cry stopped their conversation, and her breath caught in her throat. Could it be what it seemed? A tiny baby's wail? Raccoons made similar noises, but something about the insistence of this cry told her it was no animal. Eleanor walked toward the edge of the woods, and the cries became louder and more discernible. It was definitely a baby. She drew closer, but Nathaniel held her back.

"Stop, Ellie. It could be some kind of trick. Let me check first."

Eleanor pulled free. "You'll only scare the baby. Let me go."

She went to the edge of the woods, and Nathaniel held her back again. Wiggling from his grasp, she stepped gingerly into the trees. The light from the kitchen barely lit her path.

On the soft ground, rustling in the leaves, she found a black infant. The baby had been swaddled in a rough blanket.

Probably the very blanket given to the child's mother by her master when she was a child.

Eleanor picked up the baby and searched its dark brown eyes in the dim light. "Oh, Nathaniel, look." The baby blinked wildly to avoid the light, but upon seeing Eleanor's face, smiled a heartwarming grin, then promptly began crying again. "His mother must be here somewhere. Hello!" she called out. "If the baby's mother is about, please show yourself. I mean you no harm."

"She won't come with me here," Nathaniel informed her.

"Then leave," Eleanor said curtly. Seeing the hurt in Nathaniel's face, she softened her tone. "I'm sorry, Nathaniel, but this baby is so young. I want to help the mother, if possible."

"I'm not leaving you alone in the dark of night without anyone to see to your safety."

His sudden interest in her safety sent her reeling. "I've been fine for six years without you, Nathaniel. Or should I say Master Pemberton? Do you think I cannot do for myself now? Please leave—your presence is only scaring the mother." She cuddled the baby close to her, and the loud wails turned to soft, smacking whimpers. Little sniffles followed, and soon the smile returned—a precious, innocent smile that only a baby could offer.

"I'll be close by," Nathaniel announced before turning away.

Soon after, another rustling in the leaves gave way to a young girl, certainly younger than Eleanor. She had big, round eyes and clearly knew her life was in danger by showing herself at the house. Eleanor approached the girl with the baby. "Is she yours?"

The girl nodded. "He. I got nothin' to eat, Ma'am. I can't nurse him with nothin' in my bones. The men, they need food for the work, but my baby, he need it too. I wasn't going to steal nothin'. I was goin' to see if there was scraps from dinner."

Eleanor cringed at the girl's thin frame. She needed more than scraps. "What's your name?"

"Ceviche," she answered softly.

"I'll get you some food, Ceviche, on the promise that you'll come here every night. I'll leave a basket for you. You eat it here, and don't tell any of the men where you go. Do you understand?"

"Yes, Ma'am."

"Stay here. I'm going to get you and the baby a warmer blanket."

"No, Ma'am." Her eyes grew wider. "They'll know where I was if'n I come back with a blanket. The masser at Woodacre, he'll kill me for certain."

Eleanor looked at the baby and then at her mother. Of course, the girl was right about the blanket, but Eleanor feared for the cold, fall nights. Whatever the plantation owners had suffered, it was nothing next to the slaves. Looking into the depths of the mother's eyes, Eleanor could see that now. This girl had no way to protect her baby, and desperation had brought her to the edge of Eleanor's grand home in the dark of night. Could there be a more hopeless feeling? It was the first thing she would change as mistress of Woodacre.

"You're probably right about the blanket. Stay here. I'll get you some food."

Eleanor plundered through the kitchen house, avoiding the strange stares she received from the house servants. She packed the goods in a picnic basket reserved for outings on spring horse days and left without a word of explanation.

"Don't eat it too fast." She warned as she handed the basket to the girl. "And come back tomorrow for more."

The young girl held out a trembling hand but took another look at her baby and grabbed the basket. Curtseying, she ran into the dark night.

"You still feel as I do then." Nathaniel came behind her

and touched Eleanor's shoulder. It sent shivers through her spine, and she unconsciously rubbed her arms to stop the feeling.

"I don't know what you mean, Nathaniel. I saw one of God's children hungry, and I fed her. There's nothing more to it than that. She wouldn't be in such a position if it weren't for our fathers and this war."

"What will you say to my father and your future husband Andrew when they employ the black codes, Ellie? Will you sit by and watch them go against the law?"

"I shall help them write the codes if need be. They'll allow for enough food and the ability for a worker to leave should they like." Eleanor squared her shoulders, confident in her words.

But Nathaniel laughed aloud, cutting her off. "And a plot of land to call their own in the corner of the plantation.

"Tell me you aren't still so naïve, Ellie. Our fathers blame the Yankees for everything that's befallen them, and punishing the slaves is just what they've done their entire lives. Certainly your father tried to help them when your mother was alive, but what's he done for them since?"

"Freedom is the law, Nathaniel. At some point, our fathers will have to adapt. I have. I've lost everything that meant anything to me. All that's left in this house is the walls. We sold all the silver for the war effort. We even sold Mother's jewels that were sewn into my gown for protection."

"Your father let you sell your mother's things?"

"We had no choice, Nathaniel. The South gave up as much as we could to ward off the Yankees. We burned all our cotton and anything that could be considered transport so the Union wouldn't get it. We didn't want to make it any easier for them to kill Confederate soldiers."

"Eleanor, marrying my brother will not help your cause. You will only succumb to their way, their ideas."

"I haven't yet," she answered defiantly. "I've managed to stay quite grounded in my opinions, and I've helped to make the plantation workers' quarters much more livable. Imagine all I could do if mistress of both plantations. Our fathers don't understand their method won't work anymore. They don't understand that the method to continue their way of life is to treat the men well. They don't want money. They have no use for it. They want land; they want—"

Nathaniel knelt before her, grasping her hand. "Ellie, come away with me. We'll be married in Vicksburg by morning."

Eleanor yanked her hand from his touch, though it took all her strength. "You said you came home to be forgiven. Do you think anyone would offer forgiveness if you stole your brother's betrothed?" She looked deep into the hazel eyes, and she saw remorse there for his words. Eleanor reached out and touched his cheek. "I know you want to please your father, and the way to do that is to let things be. Andrew and I shall be happy, somehow. Since you've squandered your inheritance, I cannot help the slaves as your wife."

Nathaniel flinched, and Eleanor realized he understood the truth in her words. "I need Andrew as much as he needs me. It is the way of life, I suppose. Needs and desires are very different things."

"You don't want to marry my brother, Ellie. You're marrying him because you feel sorry for him. But there's nothing to pity about Andrew, Ellie. He's wanted you from the day you were born on Rosamond. He meant to make the plantations one, and he'll succeed if you give him the honor. If you think your position will help the slaves as your mother's did, you underestimate my brother."

"How dare you, Nathaniel! How dare you accuse your brother of such vile things! He loves me." But deep down she questioned her own words. How could she help but do anything less? Andrew had never whispered words of love to her. He'd never placed gentle touches upon her arm as Nathaniel did so naturally. *But that isn't love,* she told herself. Love was commitment and being there—not a passing emotion. Andrew had been there while Nathaniel flitted about the country.

"He's trained himself to love you, Ellie. Can't you see that?"

"Stop calling me that childish name. I'm not a child, Nathaniel! I'm sorry you feel your brother must be trained to love me, like a circus performer. Is it such a chore? Then why should you want to plow through life with such a dreary task?" Eleanor turned her shoulder to the man she had once loved. Every time he whispered her name she withered a bit. Did Andrew love her? Could anyone after she'd been the object of so much conjecture following Nathaniel's departure?

"I didn't mean—"

"The Nathaniel I knew would never be so cruel. I thought I knew everything about you. I agonized when you left. You showing up before my wedding is hard enough. Don't make me endure more." Eleanor wiped away a tear and tried to still her trembling frame.

Nathaniel reached for her, but she maintained her distance, trying to think of the baby she'd cradled and other more comforting thoughts of the people her marriage would help, but to no avail. She swallowed hard and looked directly into the eyes of the man she had once loved with her whole heart. As much as she feared the answer, she needed to know why Nathaniel had left.

"The town remembers how you departed. They remember me as the jilted bride, and they were right, weren't they?" She waited for the words to sink in, but he didn't answer her. "They said you escaped to avoid marrying me. They said your father had ordered it, and you wouldn't be told how to live your life. I was a laughingstock, Nathaniel, at only seventeen years of age."

Nathaniel's eyes clouded over, and Eleanor felt as though she had been struck. "It's true then? I am why you left."

Nathaniel looked away into the night's sky, and Eleanor had her answer. She marched toward the steps.

"Ellie!" Andrew's voice beckoned her.

"I must go. My fiancé calls." She blinked madly to keep the tears away. *Only a few steps,* she told herself.

As she hiked up the stairs, Nathaniel stood alone at the kitchen house, but it was she who was truly alone. Her heart ached. Nathaniel had never really loved her. He'd never loved anyone more than himself.

three

Nathaniel stood on the back stoop of Rosamond until total darkness enveloped him. One by one, the candles and the fire were extinguished in the cookhouse, and the night became blacker. Only the great house remained lit. Eleanor came into sight, and Andrew gathered her close. Pain clenched Nathaniel's heart. *You don't love her, Andrew. Let her go.*

Nathaniel closed his eyes, unable to witness his brother and Ellie together. Andrew deserved her, he supposed, but the thought caused a sour feeling in Nathaniel's stomach. Andrew stayed and fought, Andrew cared for the plantation, and Andrew stood up to be a groom, while fear sent Nathaniel bolting like a frightened catfish.

Where was he when Ellie had grown into a beautiful young woman? Had California offered him anything so special?

"Won't do you no good to stand there feeling sorry for yourself." Eleanor's childhood maid, Hattie, stood at the back step, beating a rug. She focused on her project and spoke of the decorated textile. "Surprised we got anything left after them Yankees stormed through here. A painting here and there, a rug, a few plates. We done hid the silver; they didn't get that." Hattie smiled with what appeared satisfaction.

"You think I feel sorry for myself?" Nathaniel walked toward her.

"Who wouldn't? We done all had a time of it, but thinking about it don't help none." Hattie took a stick to the rug. "Why you men can't wipe your feet outside, I never will understand."

"She's going to marry my brother."

24

Hattie shrugged. "You're just lucky she didn't do it six years ago. Consider it your penance you should watch the wedding." Hattie placed the beaten rug over the stair rail and came toward him. "Let her be, Master Pemberton. Your brother will make her happy, and the sooner things return to normal, the better. Life's been too hard for too long. A wedding will help things heal."

"Why have you stayed on, Hattie? You don't have to, you know. If things are so hard, why don't you go?"

Hattie laughed. "Where am I going to go? I got nice quarters here, and the missus taught her daughter to treat me right. I got no complaints with Miss Ellie. Mrs. Patterson, she leaves me alone for the most part. Searching for something better is what got you into trouble, Master Pemberton."

Nathaniel wanted to tell her to flee, to run now before Andrew came into possession of Rosamond, but that wasn't fair. His own prejudices probably mingled heavily into his opinions.

"No, and I don't suppose you would ever have complaints with Eleanor. She loves from the depths of her soul."

Hattie searched his eyes. "Where'd you go, Master Pemberton? Do you know how I nursed that broken heart of Miss Ellie's? We all thought she'd get over it, that she'd find someone else to love and cast off her old feelings for you like some worn-out coat. But she didn't. She wore them like a badge of honor, her own Confederate flag, waving torn in the wind. And now that you're back, she's marrying your brother. Life's odd, ain't it?"

Nathaniel thought so. "I went to California, hoping to find gold."

"Did you?"

He laughed. "It was gone a decade before I got there. I sat in grimy mining camps and finally prospected for a mining company. Any measly flake I found belonged to them."

"Did you find what you was looking for?" Hattie asked, with all the wisdom of any educated scholar.

"I beg your pardon?"

"Can't imagine what you was missing here, what with your daddy owning all that land and all. So I figured you went looking for something in particular."

Nathaniel shook his head. "I went looking for a fool's adventure, and that's exactly what I found." What *had* he been hoping to find? Everything that mattered to him was right here in Mississippi all along. Everything, that is, except adventure, and he had found that highly overrated. Wondering whether he'd make it to the next day was no longer a thrill for Nathaniel. Thinking on the American war, he probably could have found adventure in Mississippi as well. Nathaniel sighed audibly. He was no better than a dog chasing its own tail.

"What was you looking for?"

"I guess I had independence in mind, Hattie."

Hattie laughed. "Well, leaving your family high and dry is a way to find that, I suppose. I been here since I was a young girl, and I guess I never did wonder much what was beyond those white fences, so I can't fault you. Miss Ellie taught me to read, to speak properly, and how to pray to God. That's a lot to be thankful for. There ain't much more a woman asks from life but to be forgiven and know there's eternity waiting on me. That makes me happy."

Happiness. Would he ever find such an elusive thing here on earth? The Bible didn't promise it, and Nathaniel highly doubted it. "I'm glad you ask for so little in life, Hattie. I suppose that's a good way to find happiness."

"You want to know what I think?"

"I'm not sure, Hattie," Nathaniel answered with a chuckle.

"I think you're still in love with Miss Ellie, and you're planning to steal her away from your brother."

Nathaniel laughed and shook his head. "No, Hattie. Andrew's

won fair and square, and he deserves Ellie. Not that I didn't try, mind you. But Andrew will be good to her." As soon as he said the words, he knew they were untrue. Andrew had never cared for anything unless it served his own purposes. Nathaniel had no doubt that if there were any way to care for Woodacre, other than going to battle, Andrew would have found it.

As if reading his mind, Hattie went on, "You believe that, Master Pemberton?"

"No, Hattie, I really don't."

"I didn't think so. I thought you must have learned something while out in California. I pray you do steal her away, Master Pemberton, even though I could be hanged for saying so. Nothing left for a belle like her any longer. The Yankees, they treated her with the utmost respect. But the Southerners, the gentlemen, they rocked my girl's faith. They spread rumors about her and said she was on Satan's side when she tried to help a Yankee officer in need. But I know she would have helped Satan himself if he lay in a puddle of blood. Miss Ellie's like that. She's got a heart of gold. So see, Master Pemberton—you didn't need to go looking for the precious metal."

"I suppose I didn't, but I disrupted my father's plans once, Hattie. I don't plan to do it again," Nathaniel said by way of excuse, hoping he truly was being a hero letting Ellie marry Andrew. Somehow he doubted it.

"You didn't learn nothing while you was in California. Nothing. Because the Nathaniel I knew was a fighter. He wouldn't just give up the woman he loved because he didn't want to stir up any trouble, but I'm glad you've grown up. It will make things much easier."

Hattie's faith in him bolstered his own. What if God had sent him back in time for the wedding to stop it? What if *this* was God's will?

"Thank you, Hattie. You're a godsend."

Hattie laughed her boisterous, familiar laugh. "I know it. You just keep in mind what I told you."

❧

Eleanor watched Hattie carrying on below with Nathaniel. She had opened her window but could hear only muffled conversation, not the words being said. What were they discussing? No doubt it was she, but in what capacity? Had Hattie told Nathaniel to run again and leave her to be with Andrew? Her maid was far too familiar with her future brother-in-law for Eleanor's liking. And from the looks of it, Nathaniel had easily won Hattie over with his carefree style.

A knock at her door startled her from the window, and she closed it with a *crack*. She swallowed hard and opened the door. Her father stormed into the room with hands clasped behind his back. "I'm sorry to disturb you in your quarters, but Andrew has approached me with an important matter. He is anxious to get on with your lives."

"Of course, Father. That's understandable. We are to be married in a month," Eleanor agreed, hoping the direction of the conversation wasn't headed where she feared it might be.

"He's waited a long time to ensure that you wouldn't be upset by his proposal, and now that you've accepted, he's hoping to begin the marriage as soon as possible." Her staunch father patted his protruding stomach and paced the room. "When I was ready to take a wife, I was anxious to have her under my roof and begin our lives together, but there's the added issue of planting. It won't be long now, and we'll be planting. The soil will need a lot of encouragement this season."

Eleanor gulped. "Father, are you suggesting we move up the wedding? We've hardly had a decent engagement period as it is."

"No one's counting the days of an engagement anymore,

Eleanor. We've all faced death and survived. Those of us who are left must move on. What with the shelling of the town, the gunboats, no one is worried about a decent interval."

Eleanor's heart beat in her ears, and she had to think fast. The idea of marrying Andrew before she had time to prepare her heart after Nathaniel's arrival suddenly sickened her. It made her feel like the traitor she was.

"Mother would care." The comment stopped her father's pacing, and Eleanor knew she'd hit her target. His brows lowered, and he studied her. "Mother would care, Father. It's odd enough I'm marrying Andrew when everyone thought I'd marry his brother one day, but to do it quickly when Nathaniel's just returned will only intensify the gossip. People will talk, Father. Like they did when Nathaniel left— do you remember?" Eleanor looked out the window again. "I know we've always been called the proud Sentons, but I venture to guess Mother would have wanted me to have a proper engagement." She wished she could see her father's expression but dared not face him.

"I shall ask my sister for her opinion," her father said, then left without another word.

Eleanor fell to her knees as she beseeched the Lord. "I don't even know what to pray for, Lord. But please let Your will be done, and prepare my heart if I'm to marry Andrew sooner than I'd planned."

Her fate rested in her aunt Till, and, for her own sake, Eleanor hoped their opinions agreed. Hattie entered the room with a loud bang. "Are you ready to be undressed, Mistress?"

"Oh, Hattie, don't call me that."

"I'm sorry, Miss Ellie. I saw your father leave. I'm thinking about him. Everything all right?" Hattie began her nightly routine of readying Eleanor for the following day. She checked her combs and laid out an appropriate gown for the next morning. Once her ritual was complete, she turned to Eleanor and forced her eyes away.

"Why do you think Nathaniel came back, Hattie?"

Hattie clicked her tongue while motioning for Eleanor to turn around. The older woman began unbuttoning the back of Eleanor's gown and then untying her undergarments. It felt like an eternity before the maid answered. "Can't rightly say, but he means to make a name for himself here in Natchez."

"What do you mean?"

"His father has welcomed him home. That's no small gesture. Master Pemberton's going to prove himself to his father. I have no doubt."

Eleanor turned to face her maid. "Did he say anything about me?"

"Were you eavesdropping, Miss Ellie? During the war, men were shot for less."

"I knew he was out there. He approached me after dinner."

"If your father, or your future family, caught you talking with Master Pemberton, you may as well say good-bye to Woodacre. No war is going to erase that kind of scandal. Natchez hasn't forgiven him, even if his father has."

"Tell me what he said, Hattie," Eleanor begged.

"Just that he's sorry he left without word. He wants to make it up to you, but I think he knows the way to do that is to leave you be." Hattie began to pull at Eleanor's hair, letting it down from the net to fall in red cascades across her back.

Eleanor blinked back tears. "Did he say that? That he was going to leave things be?"

"It's just the way it is, Child. Propriety dictates you two stay far away from each other, and he's got a mind to make the most of his second chance at Woodacre. You wouldn't want to get in the way of that now, would you?"

"No, I suppose I wouldn't." Eleanor rubbed her temples. "I have a vicious headache."

"It's too much excitement for the day."

"I'll tell Father tomorrow that it's fine to move up the wedding. I don't suppose there's any reason to keep it a month from now. A fortnight will be plenty. I'm not as young as most to begin having children, you know." Eleanor felt somehow that if she just got her wedding over with, maybe her feelings for Andrew would follow.

Hattie began hanging up Eleanor's gowns. "You'll tell your father no such thing. Just wait, Miss Ellie. Wait and see what happens. God isn't through with you yet."

Eleanor looked into her maid's eyes and saw a certain sparkle. Although she didn't know what the elder woman had in mind, something was circulating in that head. Eleanor drew in a cleansing breath of excitement. Waiting would be the least of her problems. Getting her father and Andrew to agree to terms in hiring the slaves back at an honest day's wage—*that* was her real problem.

four

Aunt Till and her daughter Mary arrived from Louisiana the following morning. It was a bright and promising day, and Eleanor breathed in the fresh autumn air, glad to think of her future rather than her troubled past.

"Aunt Till!" Eleanor ran to the carriage without a concern for grace or propriety. Her aunt Till was finally there, and Eleanor had great expectations for her aunt's opinions on a hasty wedding. Years had passed since their last visit from her father's beloved sister, but she had little doubt how the woman would view such a societal faux pas.

Aunt Till's home had been shelled and destroyed by Yankees, but she maintained her prestige and respect even without the money usually necessary for such an honor. By all accounts, Aunt Till should have returned to Rosamond, her childhood home, a broken woman, but it hadn't happened. She had remained in Lousiana, hoping Mary would marry a handsome officer returning from the fields. Mary's beau never did return from the battles, and her heart never appeared ready to accept another in his place. Moving became unimportant in the women's shared mourning.

Aunt Till's generous frame exited the conveyance, lifting the strain of the carriage visibly. She lumbered toward her niece with arms outstretched and pulled her into a hug. "Lovely little Eleanor. Look what a beauty you have become. Your cousin Mary has been telling me of your escapades here in Mississippi."

Eleanor looked to her cousin and pen pal. Mary shook her head nominally as if to say that nothing of importance was ever relayed from the letters. Just seeing Mary made Eleanor feel like a carefree child again, wanting to giggle through the fields on her mare and jump fences behind her cousin. Eleanor grabbed Mary's hands and whispered in her ear, "I have the day all planned for us. We shall have a picnic and ride to our hearts' content."

"I heard Nathaniel's returned. Is it true?" Mary whispered excitedly. "Shall he join us as in the days of our youth?"

"Shh, no. Father has forbidden me to see him."

"So you are set to marry Andrew after all." Mary stamped her foot childishly. "I was hoping the wedding would be called off." Mary smiled sweetly to throw her mother off any trail. "Maybe not called off, but I was quite hoping for some excitement so Nathaniel might carry you off romantically, stealing you from his brother once and for all."

"What are you two conspiring?" Aunt Till asked.

"Nothing, Mother. We are discussing the wedding plans, of course."

"Ah, to be a young bride again. Eleanor, where is your father? Is he not here to greet his own sister?"

"He's in the fields, Aunt Till. He shall be back soon. There was some business to attend to, and he could not be relieved of it."

"My! Doesn't he have an overseer?"

"No, Aunt. The overseer has disappeared, but I believe he may have a new one this week." Eleanor hoped that was enough of an answer, for she knew nothing more. She had no more idea of what had happened to Mitchell Rouse than her father, but she feared for the man. He was a vicious overseer, and she couldn't say she missed him; but she also knew the men didn't miss him, and thus her uneasy feeling for him. She hoped he'd left of his own free will and hadn't met with an untimely ending.

"Disappeared, Dear?"

"Father shall tell you all about it. May Mary and I ride th
afternoon, Aunt? The servants have packed us a fine picni
and it's such a nice day."

"Mary is probably tired from our journey, Eleanor."

Aunt Till removed her gloves. Gone was the kid leather an
in its place a shiny material of lesser consequence. Eleano
winced at the sight of it.

"I'm not tired, Mother. I've never felt finer." Mary's eye
widened in her plea, and her mother relented with a smile.

"Very well, if you two should like to live your last days a
girls, who am I to stop such revelry?"

Eleanor and Mary smiled broadly, took each other's hand
and ran to the stables, giggling with glee. They fell in a hea
outside the stables, just as they had when they were childre
They laid on their backs in the tall grass, gazing dreamily a
the clouds above while their gowns stretched out beyon
them. "It is such a pleasure to be away from the house an
all its chains."

"That one looks like a tulip," Mary commented.

"And that one, a dragon," Eleanor said, pointing to the sky

Mary lifted herself onto her elbows. "How does Andre
manage without the arm? Is it very strange to watch him
I'm quite nervous I shall stare at him."

"He does fine, I suppose. I pray you won't stare at it. It
nothing really. Just his arm is not there. I guess I don't thin
of it much."

"Really? I daresay I'd be quite weary of marrying a ma
with no arm."

"Not if it was Morgan you wouldn't," Eleanor said in ref
erence to Mary's beau who had succumbed to the war.

"Andrew is *not* Morgan, Ellie. That's what I mean." Mar
gazed steadily at her cousin.

"Andrew and his father still have enough men at the pla
tation where he can tell them what work to do. Andrew ha

harsh words for the Federalists that keep a close eye on his work, though. He claims he is barely surviving, and so does my father. That's why we must forge the plantations together. I hate to hear of such matters, but I suppose it's my lot in this life. One can no longer play childish games all day. The war has put an end to that."

Mary sighed. "I don't want to discuss the war. I hate everything it represents. Let's talk of something cheerful. I'm sick of seeing Yankees lurking on every corner. Tell me about Nathaniel being back. Is he quite a criminal?" Mary said dreamily.

"You mean Andrew, my future husband. That is whom you wish to discuss," Eleanor said.

"Of course—Andrew." Mary cleared her throat. "Were you able to get fabric for a gown?"

"I'm wearing my mother's. It's the one she wears in her family portrait."

"It's such a pity she won't be here, Ellie."

It's not a bit fair. "It's probably just as well—this wedding will be small. Appropriate for the circumstances. Besides, I think she'd be disappointed I'm marrying Andrew. She never did care for him much. He was such a serious child, no fun at all. Mother always worried he'd steal the life right out of me if I was allowed to play with him."

"Will he?"

Eleanor drew in a long breath. "Andrew won't, but this plantation might. It's not like it was. There are men out of work, men who want the slaves' jobs, and Father lords that over the slaves. Or freedmen, as the Yankees call them. Things will never be the same, I suppose."

"Maybe we should have married Yankees and said goodbye to the South and all its problems. It might be nice to leave all this behind."

"Perish the thought, Mary. That's high treason." As she

said the words, she didn't know if she believed them.

Mary giggled. "Perhaps, but they did look fine in their uniforms." She winked and rose from the ground. "And don't tell me you didn't notice. Come on—let's go to the house and get our riding outfits. The horses are waiting." Mary held out a hand and helped Eleanor to her feet.

In a matter of moments, they were stripped and into their riding clothes. The speed of the horse sent a wave of exhilaration through Eleanor. It had been so long since she'd ridden free, and she pondered why. The wind in her hair wrestled with her net. She wished propriety allowed her to toss the contraption into the air. Eleanor wanted to feel this way again, to feel there was life worth living. She drew in an excited breath.

"Yah!" Mary kicked her horse and went into a full gallop.

"Yah! Yah!" Eleanor stayed with her, following closely behind. "Oh, Lord, thank You for sparing Lady!"

Most horses were stolen during the war, but Lady and her partner were kept in the slaves' quarters and spared their natural fate. Eleanor lifted an arm into the sky and wailed her enthusiasm, which brought her cousin to hilarity.

They rode to the edge of the plantation and noticed Andrew bent over the soil at the gate of Woodacre. No doubt he was wondering how the spring planting would be after a disappointing harvest this year. Eleanor wished to veer back home and avoid such painful reminders of life, but it was too late. Andrew heard the hooves, dropped the soil, and waved.

In a flash of energy, Mary jumped the fence like a professional rider and landed laughing. Eleanor couldn't decide whether to follow her cousin or halt before Woodacre's fence. She hesitated a bit too long and pulled on the reins late. Lady veered, attempting the jump, but Eleanor heard her hooves kick the fence and felt the jolt in her back. Everything happened then in slow motion, and she felt herself hurled through the air, like the firing of a cannon. She braced herself for the upcoming landing and listened in horror as Lady's body hit the ground hard.

Eleanor's twisted frame hit the soft ground with her shoulder first, and she ducked for cover at the lighted silver of Lady's shoe reflecting the sun over her. The horse fell away from her, and she clutched her chest in relief. Then she felt herself jolted by immediate gunfire, and she looked up to see Andrew blocking the sun with a pistol in his hand.

"What are you doing?" Eleanor screamed in terror. "Lady! Lady!" She ran to her horse's side, but it was too late. Andrew's gun had brought the mare to a swift ending. "Are you a lunatic?" she sobbed, grabbing her fiancé by the collar with her arm that didn't throb. "What did you do? What did you do?" She pounded her fist into his chest, and with the gun in his only hand, he was powerless to defend himself against her rage.

She felt her hands pulled behind her and Nathaniel's soothing voice calming her. "It's going to be fine, Ellie. It's going to be fine. Calm down." Nathaniel pulled her away from Andrew, locking her arms together in an embrace. An embrace meant to foil her violent reaction. "Mary, run home to Woodacre and get my father's carriage. Hurry!"

"He shot Lady!" Eleanor wailed, while seeing Andrew with more venom than she knew she possessed. She tried to free her arms, but Nathaniel held steady. "He shot Lady!"

"I'm sorry, Ellie. I'm sorry!" Andrew looked mortified, as if he was scarcely able to believe his actions. "I just reacted. Tell her, Nathaniel. Tell her I didn't mean to hurt her Lady! I'll buy you the finest mare this side of the Mason-Dixon—I promise!"

Nathaniel looked sadly at his brother. "I'll tell her, Andrew," he answered quietly.

She fell into Nathaniel's chest weeping.

"Everything's going to be fine, Ellie. We'll get you home,

and things will look different tomorrow. Andrew thought you were in danger. He tried to defend your safety."

She used her good arm to hold onto Nathaniel for comfort. "Lady," was all she could manage for an answer.

"Eleanor, is your arm okay?"

She looked down at her arm, dangling by her side. "It doesn't want to move, Nathaniel." She didn't feel any pain. She was too numb to feel anything other than the emotion of her horse lying dead beside her.

"Andrew, go see what's keeping Mary. Hurry!" Nathaniel called nervously, while smiling calmly at Eleanor. She watched as her fiancé ran toward his house, his long strides belying the weakling she suddenly felt him to be.

"Ellie, let me see your arm." Nathaniel touched her arm, and, as the shock had worn off, she flinched in pain. "It's not broken, but it's pretty badly bruised."

The arm was the least of her worries. Her horse, her one joy left in this life, was gone. Could she ever forgive Andrew? "Oh, Nathaniel, has God abandoned us?" Eleanor looked at Lady and began to sob again. Nathaniel turned her face into his chest.

"Never mind, Ellie. Never mind. This too shall pass."

"You were right to run away, Nathaniel. I wish for your sake you'd never come back to this forsaken land. There is no reason for us all to be miserable. You should have stayed away. God isn't here in the South anymore. You should have followed Him to the West. I only wish—"

"Shh. Of course, He is here, Ellie. You've just lost sight of Him. That's all. He's here, Ellie."

"Where?"

"He did what we couldn't do ourselves. Do you remember how as a child you didn't think it was fair how those children were born into ownership? You said it was just like the Israelites in Egypt—do you remember?"

"Everyone I loved has abandoned me, Nathaniel. Even you." Eleanor didn't want to think of the good the war had done. Right now, everyone was miserable. She was glad for the future generations, of course, but would those better days ever come in her lifetime?

"God has not abandoned you, Ellie." The intensity with which he said this caused her to believe him, but then she remembered her predicament.

"You'll let me marry him, Nathaniel," she said with an accusing tone. "The man who just stole the only joy I had in my life, and you'll stand by and watch me marry him. You're a traitor just like the rest of them." She hoped her vehemence would force Nathaniel into action. She wanted him to steal her away in the night, but she could see by his set jaw he had no such intentions. Eleanor pulled herself up, trying to maintain her last shred of dignity, and began the long walk home.

"Ellie, please wait. The carriage will be here shortly."

Nathaniel tried to stop her, but she'd had enough of the Pemberton clan, and she hoped to rid herself of them forever. If Nathaniel wouldn't help her, she would find a way to help herself.

five

Andrew sat in the carriage. His shoulders slumped in defeat. "She'll never forgive me."

"Of course she will," replied Mary. "She's just had a terrible time of it. Give her time to wallow in her melancholy, and our Eleanor shall return to us. Why, I'm sure by tomorrow, she'll be more herself. She is not the sort to stay in a fit."

Andrew shook his head, raking his hands through his hair. "No, no. It's different this time. Did you see her face?" Andrew relived her expression of horror, the hatred he saw in her eyes. "Did you see how she wanted Nathaniel's comfort when she stared at Lady? She never thought of me, her fiancé. I was a fool to think she'd ever love me." Andrew turned his face. "If she knew what a coward I was, she would have never said yes in the first place. I suppose I'm only getting what I deserve." Andrew knew he was being a fool, rambling on so, but he couldn't help himself. It seemed to pour from him without a thought on his part. Perhaps it was all the guilt he'd stored up for misrepresenting himself.

"A coward? Andrew, as you sit beside me with an arm missing from the war, you call yourself a coward? A prestigious medal hangs from your uniform. Your valor could never be questioned. You have just had a miserable day. Tomorrow will be brighter." Mary took his hand and grasped it in her own.

"No." Again, Andrew shook his head. "No, Mary. Things are not as they appear. I'm no soldier."

"You sit beside me wounded from the war," Mary tried to reassure him. Her eyes pitied him, and he hated the thought.

The truth rolled from him like an overfilled cotton car. "I didn't lose my arm in battle, as everyone thinks." He felt a great weight lifted from him.

"Whatever do you mean?" Mary smiled at him, obviously trying to placate his miserable ramblings, but she had no idea. She didn't know what kind of coward stared back at her.

Rumor had it Mary lost her own fiancé, a man who earned the name hero. It wasn't fair that he should be sitting here with her; it wasn't fair that her fiancé had died on a battlefield somewhere, while he was alive less an arm. Only his fear and cowardice had saved his life. Eleanor had seen the true Andrew when he shot her horse. How would he ever redeem himself now?

"I cannot say what I mean, but I wish I could, Mary. Your beau's efforts should not be in the same breath as my own. I'm not worthy. It isn't fair that I should have another chance at life while he lies in a grave."

"But God has granted you another chance, Andrew. Take it. Take it and hold onto it for all it's worth. I wish Morgan could do the same."

"I never made it to battle." Andrew admitted quietly, unable to hold the guilt at bay any longer.

"Of course you did. You were in Vicksburg. Everyone knows that. Your father is so proud; he boasts of it to everyone from what Eleanor tells me."

"No, I was thrown from my horse, Mary. I fell under the horse. His hoof landed on my arm, gangrene set in, and that's how I stand here today. I never made it to the fight. I am an expert horseman. I fear it was my own panic that threw me from that horse."

Mary's mouth opened, but she snapped it shut quickly. "I don't know what to say. I'm sure you didn't do such a thing purposely."

"There's nothing to be said, I suppose. I don't expect a

reply or understanding. But this is the reason I reacted so miserably today. When I saw that horse fly through the air, when I saw Ellie land—it was all I could do not to strangle the horse with my own hands. I suppose I blame the horse for my cowardice. I have never enjoyed riding since."

Mary exhaled deeply, clearly troubled by what she was hearing. "I cannot respond, other than to say I wish Morgan had run, Andrew. I wish he had mounted his horse, galloped the opposite way, and was here with me, known as a coward. As it is, I shall be known as a spinster, but a spinster who once loved with all her heart."

Andrew couldn't look at her, couldn't see the pain she bore. "Morgan was a fine man, Mary. I'm certain of it."

"He was," she agreed.

"Will you tell Eleanor the truth of her betrothed?" Andrew supposed it didn't matter, for Eleanor would never look at him the same way again after Lady's death. Andrew's cowardice scarcely mattered since he had killed her horse, her most prized possession.

"I shall not tell Eleanor anything presently. But you should tell her, Andrew." Mary ceased conversation at Nathaniel's appearance and presented a sweet smile to Andrew's brother.

Nathaniel noticed his brother's blanched expression immediately and felt sick to his stomach for his brother. Andrew's remorse for his actions were painted on his face as clearly as any scar; his usual, angry self-assuredness had vanished.

"We should hurry!" Nathaniel exclaimed. "Ellie has gone on ahead. She's quite shaken." Nathaniel stepped up into the carriage at Andrew's protest. "Move over, Andrew."

"You're not going with us, Nathaniel. She doesn't need you along. She's my fiancée, and I'll take care of matters."

"I'm not the one who shot her horse!" Nathaniel's words pained his brother, just as he'd meant them to, and immediately he felt the guilt. How could any Christian brother watch his brother in so much pain and feel any satisfaction? He hadn't meant to be cruel, but at the same time he wouldn't allow Andrew to focus on anyone other than Ellie. For once in his life, Andrew was going to put someone ahead of himself. "It's not me she doesn't want to see, Andrew. It pains me to remind you of that, but she's the one you need to think of. She will mend if you give her time."

"How dare you waltz back into our lives and—"

"Stop it!" Mary ordered. "Both of you are acting like spoiled children."

Of course, she was right, and Nathaniel winced at her words. He was being no better than Andrew. "Mary, you take the carriage and find Ellie. We'll wait here."

Mary stumbled over her words. "I'm afraid I don't remember the path as well as I ought to. I need one of you to come along." Mary faced them both, looking from one to the other. "Nathaniel, I think it should be you. No offense, Andrew, but Ellie would be upset at the sight of you just now. It's better if Nathaniel shows me the way. I shall relay to Ellie your concern for her."

Nathaniel breathed a quiet sigh of relief and climbed aboard the carriage. After a brief hesitation, Andrew jumped from the carriage, his face dark with anger. "Do not take advantage of me, Brother. It will be at your expense!" Andrew threatened as the red dust covered his image.

Nathaniel turned his attention to Mary. "You think it was wrong for me to return, too, don't you, Mary?" He didn't want to hear her answer but braced for it.

"I'm inclined to my opinion, Nathaniel."

"What can I do? I can't make it right with Ellie. I thought she'd be here as always when I returned. I was a fool to think of her that way. I realize that now, but I don't want her to hate me for the rest of her life. I couldn't bear it."

Mary's eyes thinned. "To think I practically worshipped

you as a child—but you're not the man I thought. Seeing you let Ellie marry Andrew, I've lost any respect I once carried for you."

"I offered myself to her, Mary. She doesn't want me. She said as much; and, besides, I'm doing what's best for everyone by bowing out. My brother will offer her the life she deserves. I can offer her nothing. I've received my inheritance and squandered it."

"Your father said he put you back in the will. At least that's what Ellie was told by her father."

"When my father passes, Andrew will see to it that the lion's share is his. And I don't care for material items, so it is of no consequence to me. I received all that I deserved and more by my father allowing me to return."

"Why did you come back then? Was it only to upset Andrew? Was it to make Ellie feel her life was incomplete somehow with your brother?"

"I came back to share my faith. I'm going to become a preacher. Perhaps it's best for everyone if I become a circuit-riding preacher and leave this place. No one listens to a prophet in their hometown—right?"

"A preacher." Mary placed a hand over her mouth and giggled, then stopped abruptly. "You're not teasing?"

"There's Ellie!"

The carriage rolled to a stop, and Nathaniel jumped out. Her eyes were red, and without a handkerchief she used the back of her hand to wipe her face. Blinking several times, she gazed at him with childlike eyes. Her russet hair was down, surrounding her shoulders and falling in gentle curls down her back. She'd never looked more beautiful to him, and he wondered if he was strong enough to leave Woodacre now. Now that he knew what he was leaving behind. Could he leave Ellie in the arms of another man? His breath left him as he pondered it.

He reached her, and she didn't fight him, as though she were discovering the same feelings. She fell against him and put her ear to his heart.

"I never thought I'd see you again. I'm so glad you came back, Nathaniel. I lied when I said you shouldn't have come. I would have wilted if I never saw you again. I think of Mary and how she felt losing Morgan. I felt nothing less not knowing where you'd gone."

"Ellie, Mary is watching."

"So let her see. Let her know that I love you. Has it ever been a secret? What else do I have to care for now? They'll marry me off as quickly as they're able. I shall be the good little wife everyone wishes. Only I will not pretend I am happy for it."

"How is your arm?" Nathaniel asked, caressing it gently with his hands. His touch caused her to flinch once again.

"Who cares about my arm? My beloved Lady is gone. You shall leave me again. If I should lose an arm like your brother, how fitting. We would be the armless couple that people come from miles around to view. Perhaps we might even join a circus."

"Eleanor!"

She pressed her hands over her face. "I'm sorry. I'm sorry. What a terrible thing to say. Forgive me. I'm not myself. You should leave Woodacre again. It's best."

"I agree," he said, breathing in the familiar scent of her hair.

She pulled away quickly, her deep brown eyes wide and fearful. "When will you leave?"

"Soon. Look at the trouble I've caused being home these few days. You and my brother will live a long life together. It will serve no purpose if I stay. I know you shall be happy without me—that Andrew is best for you." Looking into her eyes, he prayed his brother would whisper sweet words of love to her. He prayed that Andrew was entering into more than a business relationship and that he would cherish Ellie as a beloved wife, not a piece of personal property.

"I'm going to become a preacher. Perhaps a circuit-riding preacher." Nathaniel swallowed hard. He hadn't been called to be a circuit-riding preacher, but it sounded so lofty. Maybe his father would respect him if he succeeded at something other than planting. Whatever he did, he needed to get away from Ellie. Andrew deserved her; he was the one who had stayed and fought for her. And her life would be better with Andrew. He could provide her everything she was accustomed to.

"Please don't leave, Nathaniel. How will I marry him? How will I look him in the eye when I see you, and say 'I do'?" She leaned back into him, and he unconsciously surrounded her with his arms, so obviously pained by her question. It sent a wave of nausea through his stomach.

"Ellie, please don't say such things. It's not proper for you to say such things."

"What do I care of propriety, Nathaniel? My hair is down; my hoop is gone. Do I look as if I care for such manners?" She laughed, an uncomfortable, forlorn laugh. "Perhaps Mother looks down on me from her place in heaven and is encouraging me to run. I'm owned. Worse than any slave, Nathaniel. No one has set me free. I must marry whom my father tells me to marry. I'm chained to that plantation, and no Yankee law is going to help me."

"Eleanor, you are just being spoiled. Andrew will provide a nice life for you. He'll get you a grand mare, and you shall have your happiness once again. The plantations will thrive under the new laws. It will just take effort."

"Do you believe that? That I shall be happy? That a large home shall make me such?" She looked up at him, her pleading eyes begging him for the truth.

But he wouldn't give her what she asked for. It would only make things worse. He knew she wasn't spoiled or self-centered, and with him out of the picture there would be no regrets.

"Mary's going to see you home now."

Nathaniel tried to help Eleanor into the carriage, but she turned and ran. She scurried behind a collection of weeping willows. Nathaniel followed her without thinking. He found her sitting under the big tree with her arms crossed.

"We'll run together, Nathaniel. Who's to stop us? We could get married Under-the-Hill, take a ferry, and be on our way. No one questions such things now that the war has torn everything apart."

It would take one sentence from Nathaniel to silence her. He only had to say he didn't love her in such a way or that he hadn't wanted to settle down, but the words wouldn't come. They stuck in his throat like a great walnut lodged in discomfort.

"Eleanor, come and get in the carriage. A doctor should check your arm."

"Do you think your brother will treat me fairly, Nathaniel? Or do you think he wants the plantation? Tell me—does Andrew want Rosamond, or me?"

"Both, I suppose. There's no one for your father to leave it to. Why shouldn't Andrew run it?"

"There's me, Nathaniel. My father could leave the plantation to me. I would treat the men fairly, and I know just as much about running it as my father. Perhaps more because I listen."

"Ellie, I'm going home. You're talking ridiculously. I shall tell Mary where she can find you."

"Fine, Nathaniel. Leave if you must, but remember this. You do love me. I can see it in your eyes. Only yesterday you were asking for my hand in marriage, and I won't forget that. Not for as long as I live. I'll marry your brother if that's what everyone wishes for me, and I shall be a good wife to him. He is a hero to the South, and that is enough for me. But will it be for you?" Eleanor squared her shoulders. "What shall happen to you, Nathaniel?"

"Eleanor!" Eleanor's eyes opened wide at the sound of her father's bellowing voice.

"Stay here, Nathaniel. Please—my father must not know we were together."

He took her hand and grasped it. "I shall never do anything to hurt you on purpose, Ellie." He watched as her curls bounced away and then closed his eyes in agony. Her father would never accept Nathaniel as a son-in-law. He had to do what he could to make Andrew more desirable to her as a mate. It was the least he could do.

six

After two days of bed rest ordered by her father, Ellie yearned for the sunshine and the outdoors. She longed to see the magnolias and smell the Mississippi autumn. Her room felt stuffy and only furthered her feelings of capture. Mrs. Patterson hovered about Eleanor as though she were an invalid. She sighed with relief when the older woman finally disappeared downstairs to eat supper.

"Perhaps we could climb from the windows," Eleanor said with an enthusiastic grin. "Like when we were children!"

Mary answered solemnly, in a tone that reminded Eleanor they were adults now. "Your father is very concerned about you. Why would you give him more to worry over? Your arm could become worse if you don't rest it."

Eleanor exhaled deeply, knowing her cousin was right, but wanting to be childish again, if for no other reason than she would soon be married. Probably children would follow, and her carefree romps through the long grass would cease. "Another day gone. If it weren't for sneaking out in the evenings, I couldn't stand it. To think the men are free all day, and we are locked up here."

"Your father will have a fit if he finds you giving extra portions to that slave girl. You never know what dangerous characters she might bring with her one night."

"They're not slaves anymore, Mary," Eleanor said, springing out of bed and stamping her foot on the floor. No one remembered these were free men and women. "And it's time for me to get down there—the sun is nearly gone."

Eleanor packed up the remainder of her meal. She'd told the

cook she was extra hungry with her illness and had a good supply of biscuits and even portions of meat for Ceviche tonight. It would be a treat for the young girl, and Eleanor took pride in saving such a sufficient meal for Ceviche.

"My mother is in the parlor. I don't know how you'll get out tonight." Mary crossed her arms and stretched her legs onto the bed as though taking some pleasure in the thought her cousin might get caught.

"Aunt Till will be talking with her *daughter.*" Eleanor smiled and yanked Mary by the hand from her comfortable position.

"Oh, no, you've gotten me in enough trouble this week. I've already got the Pemberton boys fretting over you and asking for me to see to your every whim. Now you want me to get in between you and your father? Well, I won't do it. You're on your own if you intend to sneak out of this house. No slave girl is worth all this. My mother is right to worry after you since your father has no idea what you're capable of."

"Mary, where's your sense of adventure? Remember when we borrowed the pony to see the battle at the river? Think of all the excitement we would have missed had we stayed home as Aunt Till and Father ordered."

Eleanor hoped to persuade her cousin in her quest for freedom, which she was usually able to do. She had found her calling seeing to the needs of others, and she hoped Mary would help her do it. Nothing else felt important any longer. Not the color of her dress or the state of Rosamond or even Lady being laid to rest. Eleanor planned to help the former slaves, and she planned to enlist Nathaniel to help her. They still had that in common.

"If you won't help me, at least let me borrow your gown. Perhaps I can slip out that way. Mine are all so brightly colored."

Mary crossed her arms. "I'm not having any part of this,

Ellie. You've got no business out in the woods at night. Lord only knows what tragedies might befall you."

"Fine. Stay here, but if you heard that baby wail, you'd help her too. What right do we have as humans to starve people? I'll tell you—we've got none, Mary!"

Eleanor opened her bedroom door and peeked around the jamb. All was quiet, and she tiptoed down the stairs, leaving her cousin alone. It was the one time she remembered Mary defying what she wanted. She heard her father and aunt arguing in the library but didn't stop to listen. She was just thankful their conversation kept them so busy that they didn't notice her. It was something about the missing overseer.

She passed easily without being seen and climbed down the back steps with her basket packed. Ceviche was waiting for her at the edge of the woods as usual.

"Miss Eleanor, you's so kind." Ceviche held her baby cradled against her breast with one arm and held out the other for the basket.

"May I hold the baby?" Eleanor reached out her arms and took the infant into an embrace. Closing her eyes, she listened to the gentle smacking noises as the baby sucked on his little fingers. "He's getting so big."

"Yes'm. Now that I got me more milk, he's gonna be a big chil'." Ceviche rammed the food into her mouth and swallowed huge gulps of milk to chase it down. Her breath was labored from eating so feverishly.

"What's his name? I never asked."

"His name is Frederick. He's named after Frederick Douglass, and he's gonna be just as smart, Miss Eleanor. I'm gonna get him out of here. He's not gonna pick no cotton for his life."

"How do you know about Frederick Douglass, Ceviche?" Eleanor was mystified that anyone so remote might hear of the works of such an outspoken black man. As for Eleanor, she'd heard only derogatory statements about him from her father, but enough to know that he represented everything her father feared.

"It don't matter none. Fact is, I know." Ceviche continued to force food down herself, and Eleanor had to look away. "I also know Masser Pemberton is leaving tomorrow."

"Andrew?" Ellie turned back toward the young girl.

"Not your man, Miss Eleanor—his older brother. He's going to preach about Jesus—at least that's what he says."

"Where did you hear that?" Eleanor's eyes widened in fear that this might be the truth.

"He's packing up his things now. Andrew says it's best he leave before you's over your illness. You ill, Miss? Word is, Masser Andrew's happy to see Masser Nathaniel go. Mrs. White is helpin' him pack."

"Are you going back to Woodacre now?" Eleanor bounced the baby nervously. "Can you get a message to Nathaniel for me? A message that no one would see you bring him?"

"I can get one to Jim. Jim, he can go anywhere on Woodacre. He'd see to it that Masser Pemberton got the note."

"Wait here." Eleanor thrust back the baby and climbed the back stairs. She hunted for a piece of paper and found a bit of charcoal to write her note. She scribbled something quickly and took it to Ceviche. "Don't tell anyone you've done this."

"No, Ma'am."

"I'll see you tomorrow night, Ceviche." Eleanor bent over and kissed Frederick's head. "Get the note to Woodacre as quickly as possible."

She snuck back into the house and walked into the parlor, where her father and aunt were still having words. She acted as though she'd just come from upstairs.

"Eleanor, what are you doing out of bed?" Aunt Till stopped arguing with her father and lowered her brows in a concerned frown.

"I was thirsty. I thought I might help myself to some tea."

"Ring the bell, Eleanor. That's what it's there for." Her father crossed his arms. "Where's Mary?"

"She's in my room," she answered truthfully. "Is there any tea?"

"Eleanor, get back in your room and stay there," her father ordered.

Eleanor could see her father was in no mood for her trifling, and she promptly stood up straight and left. She closed the parlor doors, and the argument started again at once. Despite knowing better, she leaned against the wall and listened.

"Where did they find him?" Aunt Till asked.

"He was in one of the cotton fields. None of the slaves claims to know anything about it, but he didn't get there on his own."

"You've got to get Ellie married as soon as possible. It isn't safe for her to be here. She needs a husband who can keep her safe. No more of this running around on a horse between the plantations. She's had far too much freedom."

"There was a day when chivalry ruled the South. Those days are gone, I suppose."

"I'll take Mary as soon as the wedding is over, and we'll be on our way. It's not safe for her to be running about either, though she's not inclined to adventure like Eleanor. You'll need to have someone with them at all times until the wedding. It's necessary. As soon as Eleanor's arm has recovered, make arrangements with Preacher Cummings to perform the ceremony." Aunt Till clicked her tongue. "I'm so glad Eleanor's mother didn't live to see this. To see what has become of Rosamond."

"You take care of the womanly things surrounding the wedding. I'll handle the slaves, and I'll find out what happened to that overseer." Her father's voice grew louder. "Someone's going to pay with a hanging."

"Shh," Aunt Till reprimanded. "Eleanor and Mary have had a hard enough time of it. They needn't know any of this."

Eleanor clutched her hands to her chest and ran up the stairs, afraid to hear anymore. It served her right for eavesdropping. The overseer wasn't coming back. With fear and trembling she recalled running to the edge of the woods alone each night. Would she be able to go tomorrow? Or ever again? The thought of baby Frederick looking bigger and healthier drove her. She would have to find a way.

≈

Nathaniel closed his traveling pack on the small amount of items he intended to take with him. Mrs. White offered to send a food basket along, and he graciously accepted. He didn't know where he was headed or how long it might take him to find his way. He turned his face to the ornate ceiling and asked for the Lord's guidance. Andrew stood with arm in his pocket, studying everything Nathaniel did.

"So it looks as though you have everything. You should leave tonight."

"I plan to wait for daylight, Andrew." Nathaniel excused Mrs. White and faced his brother. "You have your whole life with Eleanor. You needn't worry about how soon I go. Your wedding shall be soon enough."

"Eleanor doesn't love you, Nathaniel. You squelched any of those feelings the day you abandoned her and left her to be gossiped about as a terminal spinster. I hope you don't leave thinking you're doing me any kind of favor."

"On the contrary. I'm leaving to do Ellie a favor. You two should have Woodacre to yourselves, instead of extra relatives bumbling about. Father will see to it Ellie is given the proper beginnings of your marriage, and so will I. It's only right that a married couple start out on the right foot."

"Don't ignore my words, Brother. Eleanor is not your Ellie any longer, and I'd appreciate it if you spoke of my fiancée in appropriate terms. She shall be your sister-in-law in less than a week. I'll find her a new horse, and all will be right again."

Nathaniel looked at his case before buckling it up. "I meant nothing by it, on my honor. I was only referring to my childhood playmate. I wish that you would get over this anger you have toward me. You are the only brother I have. I'm leaving, so let it be on good terms. You shall have Father and Eleanor all to yourself again. I needed to come back to make amends, but I shall not stay. Isn't that enough for you? What more would you wish?"

Andrew tilted his head to the side, avoiding eye contact with Nathaniel. What had happened to the brother Nathaniel knew? The boy who had spurred him on in races and taught him to ride a horse? Where was that Andrew now? Nathaniel was certain Andrew didn't even love Ellie. He only hated to lose, and in Andrew's mind he had lost. He wouldn't be satisfied until Nathaniel was dead. At least that's what Andrew's scowl said.

"You wish me dead, do you not?" Nathaniel asked.

"I wish you were thought of as dead. Where you go is your affair."

"I'll give you a word of advice, Andrew. Buy Eleanor a special horse, one that tells her how truly sorry you are."

"I have already spoken with a top breeder—"

"Ellie—I mean, Eleanor—doesn't want a top breeder; she wants Lady. I've written down the name of the farm where Lady came from. Perhaps they'll be able to trace the line and find you a horse who's similar."

"Lady was nothing more than a rickety old mare, Nathaniel." Andrew laughed. "She was little more than food for the hounds, and you wish me to replace her?"

"You're thinking like a man and about the value of good horseflesh. Eleanor is thinking of the horse she loved. Buy her a relative of Lady's. Trust me. Just this once. I'll not steer you wrong." Nathaniel shoved the scrap of paper into his brother's pocket. Then he held out his right arm to shake his brother's hand. "I wish you the best, Brother. Make Father proud. I know you always have."

To his surprise, Andrew reached out and took his hand. "Good luck, Nathaniel."

Stepping into the hallway, Nathaniel decided to check on his horse and the small conveyance he would take with him. He was probably gathering far too much to make an honest circuit-riding preacher, but he would wait to see where God sent him before he did anything drastic. Perhaps he would find a little church to work out of. He approached the stables and was met by Jim, one of the plantation men.

"I gots a letter for Masser Pemberton." He held out the note, and Nathaniel recognized Ellie's penmanship immediately.

He unfolded the note quickly, thanking Jim for his service. Then he bowed his head in shame at the contents.

Dear Nathaniel,

I've heard rumors that you are departing us again. Tell me it isn't true! Tell me you won't leave me here to suffer alone. My father holds me here because of my arm, but I'm afraid there is something far more sinister at work. Will you leave again without bidding me good-bye? While I am held captive?

Yours affectionately,
Ellie

seven

"Nathaniel!" His father's voice jolted him from his quiet thoughts. "You're needed here. Come back in the house with me."

Nathaniel crumpled the letter into his pocket and followed his father into Woodacre. They climbed the circular staircase into his father's study. The home, while still spacious, stood sparse and empty. All its lavish furnishings had disappeared with the war. If they'd had a mother or a sister, perhaps some of it would have been replaced by now. As it was, it remained a hollow testament to destruction.

He breathed in deeply, surrounded by the smell of his father's cigars. Whatever furniture the Yankees stole, Nathaniel was sure that scent was singed into the wood. How Nathaniel would miss that spicy scent that instantly catapulted him back in years. Back to a time when he hadn't made so many mistakes and people thought of him as a man with promise. A man they'd like to see their daughters married to. Now he was the black sheep, the one who caused whispers as he passed, and certainly no one they'd be proud to call *son*. His father entered his library and closed the doors behind them.

"Sit down, Son."

Nathaniel obediently sat at the great desk, relishing the opportunity to be called son again. How grateful Nathaniel was he'd been provided such an opportunity. "What is it you need, Father? Is it something Andrew might be able to help you with?"

Nathaniel remembered his promise to the Lord. He would do nothing to undermine Andrew's authority any longer.

Nathaniel would humble himself, as the Bible taught. No matter how difficult it might be, it was best for all involved.

"No, it's not something Andrew can do."

"I'm leaving tomorrow, Father." Nathaniel watched his father shift uncomfortably, and he tried to put him at ease. "My things are packed, and I think it's best. I shall be back for visits this time, though."

"I'm asking you to stay." He shook his head and slapped his hand on the desk. "No, I'm *telling* you to stay!" It was nearly the same conversation they'd had six years earlier when Nathaniel decided he couldn't be chained any longer and ran. The similarities drove Nathaniel to hear his father out. "We need you here on the plantation."

"I can't stay, Father. Andrew is quite capable, and my staying will only frustrate him." Nathaniel prayed for strength to broach the obvious subject they had never discussed before. "Eleanor cannot rely on me, Father. She has to turn to Andrew and I fear the only way for her to do that fully is for me to leave."

"Eleanor will do as she's told. That's her father's business, not yours. You're not going to run again because of some woman. I'm asking you for a far more important motive. All our lives could depend upon it. The woman either of my sons marry is not of concern to me, other than the obvious benefit of marrying Woodacre and Rosamond."

"I can't imagine how my staying this time would make anything better." Nathaniel raked a hand through his hair, agitated at the uncomfortable position in which his father was placing him.

"You're soft on the slaves, aren't you? Least that's what they think." His father stood and walked around the desk, sitting on it in front of Nathaniel. "They found Rosamond's overseer, Mitchell Rouse, in a cotton field. They don't know how he got there, but my fear is an uprising. Andrew's been overseeing the workers with a rough hand. I fear it might come back to haunt us."

Nathaniel clicked his tongue. "So treat them right, Father. You don't have to fool anyone if you just treat the men as they should be treated. We're to love our neighbors as ourselves."

"I fear it's too late for that. Look at Mitchell's untimely end. He was a man of thirty, perhaps. What if his death was—well, what if he was killed?" The senior Pemberton could barely utter the words.

Nathaniel knew his father needed comfort, not his anger, over how Andrew had seen to things. Guilt gripped him. How could he leave the plantation in his brother's hands? His father's fears might well become a reality with Andrew at the helm.

"Overseeing is hard work," Nathaniel stated. "I didn't know the man, but perhaps this Rouse fellow filled himself too full with drink before work. It could have been a stray Yankee looking for a meal, Father. Either way—fear is not of the Lord. It won't do us any good to be fearful. All this trouble could be solved by giving the men enough food portions to do their work. Eliminate these black codes you've started. They're nothing short of slavery, Father, and slavery is illegal. Going against the law will only harm Woodacre in the long run."

His father's wrath was stirred. "This plantation has been in Pemberton hands for generations. You think I'll have some Yankee telling me how to run it?"

His face reddened, and he clutched his chest. Nathaniel stood and steadied him.

"Father, you're getting too upset. Sit down."

He choked out the words: "You'll stay."

"I'll pray over it," Nathaniel replied. "I'll have Mrs. White bring you some tea. Have one of your cigars." He went to his father's humidor, a luxury that had obviously been salvaged, and took out a long, brown cylinder, handing it to his father.

"Pray?" His father asked. "Your family home is in jeopardy. Our very lives may depend on your being here, and you tell me you'll pray? What kind of preaching got into you in that forsaken land? Religion is for weaklings, Nathaniel."

"I've been weak, Father. The Lord is for those who need strength."

His father grunted, and Nathaniel knew it was best to abandon this line of conversation.

"What makes you suspect Mr. Rouse met with an untimely death?" Nathaniel asked calmly, unwilling to discuss his prayer life when his father was so angry.

"He was found in the field with a bottle of drink beside him. He'd been missing for over a week." The senior Pemberton ran the cigar under his nostrils, breathing in deeply. He didn't light the cigar, only savored the smell. "Rouse wasn't a popular man."

"Name me an overseer Master Senton has hired who was popular. Eleanor's father has always ruled with an iron fist, Father. No one's disappeared yet."

"Now that the Yankees got it in their heads that these men are free—well, there's no telling what will happen."

"They are free, Father."

"Your brother keeps close tabs on what the men eat. It will be no secret to the slaves who it was who ordered the portions." His father's voice was weak. "If you leave, I fear your brother may be next."

Nathaniel closed his eyes and dropped his head into his hands. *Lord, what are You telling me? If I don't go, Andrew and Ellie may never have the marriage they need. But if I go, Andrew's and Ellie's lives may be in peril.*

Nathaniel excused himself and made no commitments. He would talk to Jim and find out if the slaves knew anything before he reacted rashly.

"Wait on Him. Wait on Him," he repeated aloud to himself as he entered the hallway.

"They teach you to talk to yourself in the West?" Mrs. White held a silver tea tray and smiled at him. "Your father's expecting tea. Will you join him?"

"I'm leaving, Mrs. White, but thank you. I need to go into the fields for a bit."

"Is it safe?" she asked fearfully.

"I don't know what superstitions you've been filling your head with, Mrs. White, but it's perfectly safe to be in the fields."

Nathaniel nodded his good-bye and closed the door behind him. Outside, he mounted a horse and rode to Rosamond as if chased by a great fire. He needed to be close to Eleanor if only to ensure her safety; even if he never spoke to her again, he would see she was taken care of properly. Her nightly escapades to bring food to Ceviche weren't safe, though Ellie wouldn't care if she could help a wounded soul.

Riding to the edge of the wooded area, he saw her illumined by the light streaming out of the kitchen window. She was huddled next to a wrought-iron bench in the garden.

"Ellie!" He ran to her side, putting his arms about her. She shivered at his touch. "You're frozen to the core." He removed his coat and wrapped it around her shoulders. "What are you doing out here?"

"Ceviche told me you were leaving. It's true, isn't it?" Ellie's red-rimmed eyes looked at him.

He felt like the ultimate betrayer at the sight, and his natural instinct wanted to comfort her.

"My father is asking that I stay. I'm praying over the matter."

"Your brother was here earlier. He's asked that we move the wedding up. Was that your idea?"

"Andrew was here?"

Eleanor nodded. Again her hair was down in luxurious

curls, and Nathaniel thought he would languish over the intimate sight. It took all of his willpower to keep his hands from caressing the locks and feeling the silky strands between his fingers.

"He kissed me," she said shamefully. "Not the kind of kiss you and I ever shared, Nathaniel. It hurt."

Nathaniel clenched his fists tightly, and his jaw tightened in anger. "What do you mean he kissed you, Ellie?"

She shook her head. "I don't want to talk about it. It was awful, Nathaniel. Is that what marriage is like? I always thought it would be like that idyllic way I felt when I saw you run across the field. You know, that sweet, butterfly feeling in my stomach. But it is not going to be like that, is it, Nathaniel?" Her wide coffee-colored eyes blinked at him, looking for hope in his answer. "I thought a woman could make herself love any man she chose as her husband, but that heavenly swirl in my stomach won't ever come with Andrew, will it, Nathaniel?"

"Ellie, I don't want you coming out here alone anymore."

"I don't want to be married to a man who kisses me like that," Eleanor whispered, almost to herself.

Nathaniel's gut turned at the innocence in her voice. He would see his brother dead before he would let him touch Ellie harshly again. He closed his eyes, remembering his vow before God. He was supposed to help Andrew be a proper husband to her. Was that possible?

"Did you hear me, Ellie? It's not safe for you to be here alone anymore. You stay in your room. Tell your father you still don't feel well, but stay there until you hear from me. I'll send a pebble to your window when I return."

"Where are you going?" she asked, her voice shaking.

"I'm going Under-the-Hill to ask a few questions." Nathaniel couldn't be more specific than that. It was bad enough he admitted to going where the bars and brothels thrived.

"Why must you go there?"

"It's something I must do."

"You are coming back, aren't you, Nathaniel? You won't leave me again? I won't hear from Ceviche that you've abandoned us?"

"Ellie, don't look at me as if I was born to deceive you. It's not like that. You know I have to do what I must. You know that Rosamond and Woodacre need each other to survive."

Nathaniel couldn't look at her when he said the words. How could he tell her it was all right to marry a man who made her feel ill? That she wasn't entitled to a man who made her stomach swirl sweetly? How could he tell her the very sight of her sent his own heart racing and made him want to forget any vow he'd ever made?

"Nathaniel, will you kiss me?" Eleanor's face was mere inches from his own, and he felt her warmth to his inner soul. But sin felt good before one committed it. "My stomach is swimming now. I need to know if it only feels that way for you."

Nathaniel stood abruptly. "No, Ellie, I won't. You're my brother's intended bride. This is wrong."

She stood beside him, leaving her hair to whip around in a way that reminded him of all he might lose. "You're going to change that, aren't you, Nathaniel? You're not going to let me marry him." Eleanor pressed her cheek against his chest, and he knew his pounding heart betrayed his calm front.

"Stay in your room, Ellie. I'm promising you nothing." Nathaniel turned on his heel and didn't look back for fear she would know what he really felt.

eight

Eleanor forgot to breathe as Nathaniel's horse drove into the dark night. It seemed she had spent a lifetime watching Nathaniel leave. Always wondering if this was the time he would never return to her. It never got any easier to watch him go, but she was resigned to it now. One day it would be forever, and it was time she got used to the idea. She stood and walked to the back porch.

"Ellie?" Mary's hand touched her back gently. "Hattie is up in your room. She's been putting off Aunt Till. But I fear your days are numbered if you don't come in now. You don't want them to know about you feeding the slave girl, do you?"

"I'm coming."

"What's happened?" Mary's tender voice caused a flurry of emotion. The tears began again for Eleanor, and she embraced her cousin.

"I'm not going to marry Nathaniel," she said, by way of recognizing the fact.

"No, Ellie, you are not," Mary answered gently. "It is for the best."

"You seem to like my fiancé. Tell me why." Eleanor hoped that hearing something positive about Andrew would help her focus on him and not on the slim chance of Nathaniel's returning to her. Woodacre and Rosamond's future depended upon this marriage. Nathaniel's reputation was scurrilous. She was engaged to marry his brother, and her father would never put their beloved plantation in the hands of a Yankee.

Her father, Master Senton, called anyone who didn't help with the war effort a Yankee, because if you did not help, you hindered. Nathaniel was the coward who had left his family, and nothing would change that in her father's eyes. As the wedding loomed, Eleanor's hopes diminished. Seeing Nathaniel again was only torture to her wounded heart.

"Andrew is not Nathaniel, Ellie. He will not run at the first sign of trouble. He'll save your land," Mary said brightly, and Eleanor realized she'd been speaking. "He's serious and thinks more of the future than Nathaniel does. He will provide a good life for you. You cannot compare the two brothers. It's like comparing cotton with tobacco." Mary squeezed Eleanor's hand for reassurance.

Eleanor wished she had her cousin's sense, but she wore her heart out in the open. Hiding her feelings would come soon enough. "How can I help but compare them?"

Mary seemed to search her mental libraries for something good to say about Andrew. She did not take nearly as long as Eleanor might have. "Andrew is handsome and dashing if you'd only see him that way, Ellie. He is a proud Confederate warrior, with medals to prove it. I'll admit Andrew has lived in Nathaniel's shadow, but he's a fine man. I know any number of women who should be happy to call him their husband."

Eleanor recalled the harsh kiss he had planted upon her and couldn't imagine ever being happy for the opportunity. "Do you know such women?" she asked sincerely.

"I do," Mary answered. Her words were slow and deliberate. "Andrew loves you, Eleanor. He'll be a good husband. I know I've always been partial to Nathaniel, but who hasn't? And this trip I'm wondering if I hadn't made a mistake in that. Nathaniel is easy to love, I'll grant you that, but Andrew is steady and true."

"Steady? It sounds as though you're describing a field horse, Mary." Eleanor couldn't help herself; she giggled like a schoolgirl. It felt like the finest luxury to laugh through her tears. "Surely you can think of something better to say of my fiancé than he is steady."

"I can say he is alive, Ellie. Which is more than I can say for my dear Morgan. You are blessed to have a decision of any kind. I had none. Death took my love from me, and I shall have to wait to hold his hand in heaven."

"You think I have a decision?" Eleanor stifled a shudder. She wondered if Mary might see things differently had she been the recipient of Andrew's harsh kiss. "I'm so sorry about Morgan, Mary. It's not right that you should have lost him, but so far you've told me my fiancé is steady and alive. It's not exactly the feelings that inspire passion in a woman."

"Passion is exaggerated in importance, Ellie. It shall cease. That's what my mother says."

"I should hope it doesn't. Maybe I am a fool, Mary, but I would rather have a fleeting year of passion than a lifetime of *steady*. What is there to a dull, fixed life? Especially after the excitement of the war, I fear I will not be content as a wife. I have watched shells fly by my family home. How can I live with dull? I wish my mother were here to question on the matter. She would tell me if I was doing the proper thing."

Mary sighed. "I long for a steadfast life. How sick I am of the ups and downs, the riches and poverty, the starvation and plenty. I should love to live a simple life with a steady husband, but I fear Mother would be lonely without me at her side."

"You do not think you'll ever marry then?" Eleanor wrinkled her face, confused at the notion. It seemed she had no other options besides marriage, and here Mary sat free from the prospect because her fiancé had been lost to the war. Eleanor's true love had disappeared to the West. Why was she expected to marry?

"Now that the prospects for marriage have dwindled so, I must say I doubt it. I never was as popular as you are with the opposite sex, and since there are so many women fairer than I, my chances are slim. I fear I don't have the lush curls and batting eyelashes men seem to favor. Morgan was different. He was attracted to my intellect. He thrived in it, but I'm afraid most men find a bookworm useless in this time of our history."

"You survived, Mary. And don't forget it. God has put us here for a reason, and we have to believe He has a plan. I'm only lamenting that His plan may not match mine. It's selfish of me, I admit." Eleanor hoped to encourage her cousin. "But how like God that is, and He always seems to wrap His gifts so much prettier than I ever could. His hands stretched over darkness and created the world. I suppose I cannot question what He has for me now." She knew her words were never truer, although she had been selfish in her pursuits.

"I suppose I cannot question God in this."

"I wish I wasn't at the mercy of my father. He thinks only of the plantation since Mother died. He'll not care if Andrew is a suitable match for me."

"I don't think that's true, Ellie. Your father loves you. He wants to see you well taken care of after his death. That's a noble trait, and remember Who put him in charge of your life."

"Let's not talk of sad things any longer. I'm to have a new gown for after the wedding. Would you like to see the pattern I've cut?"

"I'd love to! I'm so glad we shall be able to create gowns and have fabrics of luxury once more. What a mean spirit those Yankees must have had to come in and destroy our gowns for sport and our china for target practice. Have they no shame to go into a woman's bedroom and tear through her things?"

"Let God be their judge. I'm just glad they're gone. Once we combine the plantations, things will be normal again. We'll have cotton and fabrics and food and servants. We shall even replace things that have been lost."

Eleanor forced a note of cheer to her voice. Maybe things would be better as she said. She looked at her cousin and saw the melancholy there. Immediately, she chastised herself for her careless talk.

"I'm sorry, Mary. I know things will never be the same for you. Not with Morgan gone. How thoughtless of me to say such a thing."

Eleanor thought she heard a horse's hooves and looked into the dark night, but only blackness stared back at her.

"Never mind, Ellie. Never mind," Mary said, and Eleanor was left to wonder if she referred to the night sounds or the loss of Morgan.

&

Long before Nathaniel reached the infamous Under-the-Hill port, he could hear the raucous noise from Silver Street. Its brick buildings teemed with sailors, drunkards, and bandits. Nearly every night someone was murdered, and Nathaniel prayed tonight wasn't his night as the boisterous sounds came closer. It was a dark night with no moon in sight, and the Mississippi appeared as only deep blackness. But Nathaniel knew it was there. He could hear the echo of drunken men's voices bouncing off the calm waters.

The vile scent of the town, something like coal, molasses, and foul liquor, mingled under his nose. Slowing his horse to a trot, he prepared to step into Mississippi's underworld. He hoped his intuition was wrong, that Andrew had no business here.

As he came onto Silver Street, the noisy tin pianos and fiddles belted his senses. Women offered themselves to him from the boardwalk with a coquettish nod of the head. Nathaniel turned his eyes away, disgusted by the overt display. Rabble-rousers lined the streets, yelling obscenities as he passed. He ignored everything until he reached his destination.

He climbed from his horse and paid a man, who looked as

respectable as any he'd seen on Silver Street, to watch his horse, offering more if it was there when he returned. Luckily, horse thievery was still punishable by death, and even drunk men weren't likely to play with such a heavy sentence. Nathaniel entered the Rumbel and Wensel store, which was just another bar. But this place had nothing on the dirty mining camps of California, and Nathaniel took comfort in the fact that God was beside him.

Approaching the grocery clerk, who was a bartender at night, Nathaniel was careful not to give himself away. One sure way was to order something other than liquor, but Nathaniel had played this game before. "I'm starving. You got any grub back there?"

"I can have the missus cook you up something. You just get off a flatboat?"

"Nah. But I'm hungry just the same." Nathaniel took out some cash and flashed it. Answers were much easier to get when the prospect of making an easy dollar was obvious. "Been up to Natchez. I'm looking for a man named Mitchell Rouse. You know him?"

The man's eyes thinned, and he motioned for his wife to cook something. She hurried back to the kitchen. "What do you want to know?"

"His boss is looking for him. Ran off the job, and they want their pay back. You heard anything?"

The bartender bent toward Nathaniel, grabbing a bill for himself. "I might."

Nathaniel pulled the remainder of the cash toward him. "Word on the plantation is the slaves might have pulled a Nat Turner," Nathaniel said, referring to the slave who pulled a revolt killing several owners and their families. The story was infamous, and many owners ruled with an iron fist out of fear that such a thing could happen to them. Nathaniel wanted to offer something to the bartender to throw the man off any trail of his identity.

"Slaves most likely got nothing to do with it." The bartender looked around him before resuming his wiping of the counter. "Rouse was here about a week ago. He was fighting with a man over a shipping tax."

"What would an overseer have to do with a tariff?" Nathaniel froze at the slipup. No street dweller would use such a term, but the bartender didn't seem to notice. The man was still salivating over the dollar bills in Nathaniel's possession.

"He wasn't just an overseer, from what I hear. He ran a business here at night. A certain business dealing in trade, if you know what I mean." The man motioned with his brows and looked to a nearby woman drinking with a patron.

Nathaniel's stomach turned at the thought of dealing in human flesh, and it took all his willpower to keep his disgust from showing in his expression. "Ah," Nathaniel said casually.

"When a man don't pay the tax, his haul gets confiscated. No goods, no cash. No cash, your credit catches up with you, if you know what I mean. Rouse probably threatened the wrong man."

"You think Rouse is dead?" Nathaniel feigned ignorance, knowing the man had been lying in his cotton field the day before.

"That's what the man said. You're the second guy who's been here looking for him today. Some one-armed guy was here this afternoon saying Rouse was dead. Was there any kin?"

"One-armed?" Nathaniel was stunned at the description of his brother.

"He acted like he didn't know what Rouse was up to, but I seen him in here before. He knew why Rouse was dead; he just wanted to know who did it." The bartender dried a glass, and his wife appeared with a plate full of potatoes under a slop of gravy.

Nathaniel smiled at the woman. "Do you know who did it?" he asked the bartender.

"I got my ideas. But you ask that one-armed guy. He knows more than he's saying. I can taste it."

Nathaniel handed the man three dollars and started in on the feast before him.

nine

Doctor Hayes glanced over his spectacles. "Your arm looks fine, Miss Senton. I'll tell your father you are cured." He stood up, placing his instruments back in his bag. "Anxious to be married, I suppose?" He smiled at her as though she were a lovesick girl waiting for a happy diagnosis.

"What about the color of my arm? Will it go away?" Eleanor asked, hoping to remind the doctor and those concerned that her arm still looked like a ripe blueberry. Surely, no doctor would approve such a vicious bruise on a bride.

"Give it a few weeks," he answered. "A long-sleeved gown will take care of it presently."

Eleanor faltered at the advice. A long-sleeved gown wouldn't hide her heart, which seemed to beat only at the sight of Nathaniel. At least that was the only time she noticed she had a heart, when it thundered as he approached. Her quiet night jolted her back to the present. No pebbles were thrown at the window, although she couldn't sleep for thinking she might miss Nathaniel. Perhaps this was the time he had gone for good.

"I'll see myself out, Hattie. She may get into her hoop contraption and rejoin the land of the living," Doctor Hayes advised.

Eleanor blushed red at the thought of this man discussing her hoop, but she dismissed it. Chivalry hadn't been the same since the war. It probably never would be. Suddenly, the thought struck her as funny, and she giggled out loud.

Mary came to her side. "Whatever is so funny, Ellie?"

"The war has certainly changed things. Doc Hayes has

72

commented on my hoops. I daresay he wouldn't mention such things before. I guess we have all seen too much."

"Andrew is downstairs. He wishes to speak with you."

Eleanor swallowed hard, and the folly immediately left her voice. "Andrew?"

"Yes, Andrew, your *fiancé*. I think he may have discussed the wedding date with your father. They seem to be in quite good spirits."

Now Eleanor's heart beat rapidly, but it wasn't the pleasant feeling she anticipated. It was fear. Chances were, she would be married before she ever saw Nathaniel again, and the answers he went searching for would serve them no purpose. After tightening her corset and fastening her hoop, Eleanor checked her reflection in the mirror and practiced a smile. She clenched and grimaced until she saw teeth. When she was satisfied with her playacting, she started down the circular staircase. Her father and Andrew waited in the foyer, and the closer she got, the farther away they both felt. When she stood beside them, it was as though another body had taken her place.

Andrew smiled pleasantly enough, and Eleanor again forced her lips in an upward fashion. "Hello, Andrew."

"I have a surprise for you, Miss Eleanor." Andrew clicked his heels together and motioned toward the door.

He followed Eleanor out, and her eyes opened wide, hoping it was not a mere figment of her imagination. Her jaw dropped at the sight of a horse that appeared identical to Lady. She was a chestnut beauty with a black mane, and Eleanor instinctively went toward her.

"She's beautiful!" Eleanor exclaimed, patting the dark mane. "Whose is she?"

"She's yours. A cousin of Lady's. I purchased her from the same horse breeder."

"You did?" Eleanor was taken aback.

This was something she could appreciate about Andrew. He had figured out where Lady came from and purchased a family member. She looked to the horse's deep brown eyes and felt a bond. Lady lived on in this mare. She ran to her fiancé and threw her arms about him.

"I'm speechless, Andrew. I don't know how to show my gratitude. No one's ever given me a more thoughtful gift."

She smiled and noticed Andrew's shy, sheepish grin. This was the kind of gift Nathaniel would have given her. She shook the thought from her head. Perhaps she'd been too harsh on Andrew. This proved he was more than steady, and it was time she started focusing on the future, not her past. Nathaniel was her past.

"Thank you," she managed. "I'm sorry I was so emotional and uncivil the day of my accident."

"Never mind, Eleanor. You deserve this horse. I wish you understood how sorry, how truly sorry, I am about Lady." Andrew bowed. "This mare has been broken. Are you ready to ride her?"

Eleanor brightened. "I can hardly wait." She dashed up the stairs, with Mary at her heels. "Oh, Mary, can you believe she's such a fine mare? I wish it were Lady, of course. But I shan't act spoiled anymore when Andrew has done me such a service. I should be truly grateful for such a beautiful horse, and I shall be."

Eleanor ran to her room where Hattie was spreading out her dinner gown. "Hattie, forget about that gown. I need my riding clothes. I have a new horse!"

"A new horse?" Hattie questioned. Eleanor knew her father didn't have the money for such luxuries right now, and probably Hattie did as well. "You haven't got time to gallivant before dinner."

"It's a wedding gift—from Andrew," Eleanor explained.

"A gift? Is that what they call it when a man replaces what

he shot?" Hattie mumbled.

Eleanor's gaze fell, her spirits sinking like a spent gunboat to the bottom of the mighty Mississippi.

"He *had* to shoot Lady, Hattie. Her leg was broken most likely, wasn't it, Mary?" She looked to her cousin—to someone who could make her believe things weren't that bad. Mary's eyes flickered and strayed about the room. Her eyes focused everywhere but on Eleanor. "Right, Mary? He *had* to shoot Lady. He's a hero. Tell Hattie, Mary."

But Mary didn't answer, and Eleanor looked at Hattie's disapproving scowl.

"Rosamond is going to go to the codes, Miss Ellie. Make no mistake about it," Hattie stated, as though it were a known fact.

"What does my new horse have to do with that?"

"If a horse can make you forget what you've been fighting for—"

"No, Hattie. There will be no codes here. Father will see to it that the men are given their freedom. Mississippi may not see them as people, but Father does. I know he does, Hattie. Rosamond would never turn to the black codes. It's simply another form of slavery, and Father never treated his men like that."

"That may well be true, Miss Ellie, but when Master Pemberton owns things, things are going to change."

Mary interrupted. "I think you've stated your opinions quite plainly, Hattie. That's enough."

"It won't. You have my word on it," Eleanor protested.

"Your word. Has your word stopped you from feeding that poor starving girl from Woodacre? I know what you are doing, Missy. I didn't raise you from an infant to be fooled by your nightly exits from this house. Why do you think she's coming here if things are so good at the Pemberton house?"

Eleanor felt the blood drain from her face. She had meant

for her marriage to solve problems, not create different, worse problems. Looking at Mary and Hattie, she suddenly felt as if she were a traitor, and that her new horse had chains draping from its hindquarters.

☙

Nathaniel sat on the docks watching as the flatboats and paddle wheelers maneuvered around the Port of Natchez. It had been a long night, and Nathaniel wasn't any closer to learning the truth about Mitchell Rouse than he'd been the night before. Nathaniel rubbed the back of his kinked neck and tried to stretch out his tired shoulders. On the trail for Rouse, Nathaniel had discovered something unsavory about Andrew's dealings. Woodacre wasn't nearly as bad off as Rosamond, and Nathaniel had thought it was Andrew's tight ledgers. But now he wondered. While most Southerners had burned their cotton rather than let the Yankees get it, Andrew had sold theirs at a healthy profit, not caring who purchased it. Had he done worse?

If the town knew of these scalawag dealings, Woodacre's reputation would be dashed. It was one thing that Nathaniel had tarnished the family name by "running" rather than fighting in the War between the States, but to know Andrew may have profited from the South's misfortune would seal their fate forever. In the future no one would do business with Woodacre knowing they were scalawags. It was worse than the carpetbaggers of the North.

"Who you lookin' fer?" A gruff voice met him, and Nathaniel looked up, thinking Goliath lived again. A huge beast of a man blocked the sun completely, and Nathaniel stood up for fear of getting trounced upon.

"I'm waiting for Jeremiah Coleman. You know him?" Nathaniel stammered.

"What d'ya want with him?"

"I want to know what business he's had with Mitchell

Rouse." There was no sense playing cat and mouse with this man. Nathaniel knew decidedly who would lose.

The man laughed and spit tobacco into the water. "There's a name I haven't heard for awhile. I'm a seaman, Mister. Don't do nothing but haul cotton and molasses upstream." The man walked toward his flatboat, which had just docked, and heaved a box onto the dock.

"Did you haul cotton for Rouse?"

"Maybe some. Who wants to know?" The man turned and held a meaty palm upward, and Nathaniel obliged with a five-dollar bill.

"Nathaniel Pemberton."

The man looked him up and down and crossed his arms. Then he laughed. "You're most likely related to the one-armed Pemberton? Why don't you ask him?" Jeremiah dropped his box, and the dock shook with the action.

"I'd rather hear it from you, if you got a notion to talk." Nathaniel took out a wad of bills and fanned through them. He watched the man lick his chops and wipe away the remaining saliva.

Jeremiah nodded. "What's the one-armed scalawag to you?"

"He's my brother," Nathaniel admitted.

"Ah," Jeremiah noted. "You're the deserter."

"I left before the war."

Jeremiah's eyes widened in disbelief. "I ain't your judge, Boy. Tell it to God."

"God's forgiven me," Nathaniel said, thankful for the chance to be bold in his faith.

"Yeah, but your brother ain't." Jeremiah laughed. "I can't say I care much for that brother of yours. He'd just as soon cheat you as look at you. Losing his arm didn't do anything for his soul."

Nathaniel swallowed uncomfortably at the thought. His brother lived for himself. Would he ever humble himself to

God? "So does that mean you're willing to talk?"

Jeremiah handed back the five-dollar bill. "I'll tell you what you want to know, Pemberton. You're a fellow brother in the Lord, and I got allegiance to Him." Jeremiah looked up to the blue sky, and Nathaniel nearly fell backward at his luck. "What do you want to know?"

ten

"Mary, please tell me. I know you." Eleanor pleaded with her cousin, her palms sticky from her desperation. "You know something you're not divulging. If I should marry Andrew and some dark secret should come about, some dark secret that you have knowledge of, what then? Will your guilt haunt you like a field ghost for the rest of your days? This is for you, as well as for me." If there was a way out of this predicament, Eleanor wanted to know it. How dare her cousin stand in her way!

Mary pursed her lips and gnawed on them a bit before speaking. "I gave my word, Eleanor. Someone not holding his word is what killed my Morgan. If the Yankees hadn't known his men were advancing, he might be alive today." Mary shook her head rapidly. "I won't do it."

"So you are willing for me to embark on a marriage such as this one, while you hold this secret to your breast." Eleanor used every tactic she knew to try to break Mary, but nothing worked. At this moment, she hated the fact that her cousin had such character and devotion to the South. Where was Mary's devotion to her? Where was their sisterhood?

"If I thought you were in any kind of danger, I would divulge my secret without a care, but you are not in any danger, Ellie. My secret is of the past, not your future."

"But the Negroes might be in danger, Mary. Will your conscience allow them to suffer? I have worked hard to see that Father complied with the new laws without harming the plantation."

"What I know has nothing to do with Andrew's running of the plantation. I know nothing of such things. You can rest

79

easy, my dear cousin." Mary bent over her knitting, her sterling silver needles clanking wildly as she worked.

"But I cannot rest easy, Mary. Downstairs beckons a beautiful horse, and she is calling my name and my future. Do you know of a reason I shouldn't accept such a present?"

"Hattie's just talking, Ellie. She is just trying to make trouble, and she is overstepping her boundaries."

Mary looked at Hattie, and the older woman nodded her head slowly.

"You all keep me out of it," Hattie said, "if you know so much."

"Hattie!" Eleanor exclaimed. "Do you know what Mary knows?"

"I don't know anything but my feelings, and my own feelings say that horse is poison. Anything that man touches is poison. Rosamond will be next. That's all I'm saying."

"Hattie," Mary chastised, "Eleanor is going to marry this man. You need to mind your place."

Hattie went about the room, straightening up. She closed her lips firmly over her teeth and said nothing more, but Eleanor understood her silence. Her silence meant Eleanor was a traitor to Nathaniel. A betrayer to Rosamond, the Negroes, and her, and it was how Eleanor felt. The beautiful mare was only a bandage to the pain. It would do nothing to heal her hurts or mistrust of the man she was soon to call her husband.

Mary dropped her needles to her lap. "Very well. I will not tell you the exact knowledge I carry, but I will tell you Andrew is not what he seems. That is not to say I think he is of poor character, however. I believe he would make a fine husband for you, Eleanor." Mary looked at Hattie with a scowl. "Would you like it if she should be a spinster like me, Hattie? Nathaniel certainly isn't fit to marry. He hasn't two pennies to his name and no more right to Woodacre than you or I. Would you rather she marry him?"

"Yes." Hattie had clearly had enough and bolted from the room, slamming the door behind her.

Eleanor had never silenced Hattie in the past, and Mary's insolence because of Hattie's color obviously perturbed the elder woman to no end. And with good cause. Eleanor had always been taught to respect Hattie and that, no matter what happened, Hattie would always tell her the truth.

"That woman has more nerve." Mary sighed and looked at her cousin. "I think you should marry Andrew without reservation. I must admit, when I first stepped out of our carriage and saw Rosamond's grounds again, I thought only of you and Nathaniel together. I was so charmed by the memories of Nathaniel. But I know he can't be the same man any longer. California would have changed him. Poverty has changed him."

"Who is to say I want Nathaniel?" Eleanor crossed her arms defiantly, hoping to keep her heart to herself, but her cousin continued.

"Eleanor, haven't you lived a poor life long enough? The Yankees have done their damage, but Andrew has triumphed. Don't you want to share in that? To see Rosamond transformed into its former glory with its fine furnishings and lavish luxuries? Andrew has the means to do all of that. Nathaniel doesn't."

Did her cousin know her so little to think she thought of such trifles? Surely Mary knew honor and love were far more important than material goods. "I should think I have more character than to worry only about pretty gowns and fine furniture."

"Of course you do. You also care about the former slaves. You don't want to see them abandoned, do you? Combining Rosamond and Woodacre—"

"Is exactly what the Federals are trying to halt. President

Johnson wants to limit the size of farms so that slavery is abolished completely, including the black codes. Combining the plantations will put us under a Yankee microscope."

"It will also make you rich enough not to care, and you know it."

Eleanor did know it. Marrying Andrew was by far the easiest way to help the Negroes, but Hattie's words haunted her. What would God have her do? He would want her to help the slaves, wouldn't He? As much as she desired Nathaniel, that didn't make it God's will.

"I'm going to accept the horse, Mary. I want to ride today without a care in the world. I want to see the countryside and forget all these problems today."

Eleanor started down the stairs and met her fiancé's gaze with a happy grin. His mount stood beside hers, and she suddenly felt trapped.

"I was hoping to get to know my horse today," she said by way of excuse.

"Well, Eleanor," Andrew stammered, "it has only been a week since you fell. I'd like to be certain you are up to the ride. Besides, it isn't safe for you to be alone. A chaperone is quite necessary."

"I shan't go far. I will return before lunch—I promise."

She stepped on the foot ladder to her new mare and proudly trotted away against Andrew's protests. As soon as the shade trees covered her, she clicked the horse into a full gallop and streamed like the Mississippi. She pulled her hair from its net and shook it out so it fell down her back. The wind on her face, the scent of the magnolia, the bright green of new grass—all caused a stirring sensation within her. Every part of her felt alive and refreshed. As long as she had these moments of freedom, she could endure anything.

The sound of hooves met her, and Eleanor's heart sank. Andrew had followed her, taking her dreamy state far away.

She pulled her horse under a magnolia and stayed there, hoping Andrew would pass her by and leave her to relish her solitary ride. Her breath was labored from her run, but she patted her new friend and spoke softly to her. They were going to get along well.

The hooves sounded closer, and Eleanor tried to act as though she were only taking a rest for a moment should Andrew happen upon her. She looked up at the grand magnolia and remembered as a child her days running under these trees. She and Mary and Nathaniel would have a rousing game of hide-and-seek while Andrew looked for snails and other such discoveries. The oncoming horse slowed its pace, and Eleanor's stomach lurched joyfully at the sight of Nathaniel.

She dismounted from her horse, as did he, and she ran toward him, clutching him for what would probably be the last time. Without thinking, she kissed his rough face, running her hands over his jaw. "Nathaniel. Take me away from here." Where such bold words had come from, she did not know, but she meant them, every one.

Her words shot through him like a bullet, for he pulled back quickly. "Eleanor, don't say such scandalous things."

"We shall be married," she said, breaking every law of womanhood her mother had so laboriously taught her. "I shall become the perfect preacher's wife, Nathaniel. I will learn to cook and clean and keep a proper house. We shall find a nice little parish somewhere and settle."

"Ellie," he whispered her name. By his eyes she knew he wanted to kiss her, and she made the most of his moment of weakness. She placed her lips on his and felt the firm line of his lips return her kiss with vigor.

Again he pulled away. "Ellie, stop it! You were born to live this way on a great estate. Even the Yankees can see that. They've allowed your home to stand. They've moved upriver because they know you belong here. The *Essex* dared not interfere with you—how shall I?" Nathaniel said, referring to the gunboat that had attacked their fair city long ago. "I only ask that you stay here on Rosamond, but do not marry my brother."

"Tell me what you've learned, Nathaniel. Tell me why you've come back to me. Why you would wish for me to be alone forever."

"I don't wish for you to be alone. I just ask that you not marry my brother. I'd rather see you marry a Northerner."

"Tell me why."

"I cannot."

"Then I shall marry Andrew." Eleanor crossed her arms, but she broke under Nathaniel's gaze and fell into his broad chest. He smelled of the river, but she didn't care. She knew this might be the last time she ever held him again. "Take me with you, Nathaniel. Please."

She looked up into his hazel eyes, which were filled with tears. He tried to blink them away but could not, and she triumphed that she was breaking him. More tears appeared on the horizon of his gold-flecked eyes with each closure. "I cannot take you," he said again.

"My father will make me marry him, Nathaniel. If you leave, you leave me with Andrew. I'll have no other options to me. The black codes will be employed on Rosamond as well as Woodacre, and you will run from it. For once, Nathaniel, I ask you to be the man I know you to be."

He clutched her arms tightly. "Do you think I'm weak, Ellie? Do you think it's easy for me to leave knowing whom I leave you to? I leave because I'm strong, Ellie. And it's not my strength that propels me; it's His."

"But you'll still leave." Eleanor couldn't mask her scowl. This wasn't about getting her way. This was about their future. The legacy of their family estates. "You think Andrew is a better choice for running Woodacre than you."

"It doesn't matter what I think. My father has chosen."

"Your father didn't choose. Your father was never given the chance, Nathaniel. You left him no choice when you packed up for California. Give him a choice now. For all our sakes. Mary knows something of Andrew; you know something of him. All of you keep your secrets while you leave me as the sacrifice."

"Better I leave you than stay. That you resent me now than later when we must raise our children in the washhouse, with only a spinning wheel and loom as our furnishings. When you have a baby on your hip and an iron in your hand, would you still find me so wonderful? I have nothing to offer you, Ellie."

"You have yourself, Nathaniel. Why does everyone think I care for things? I watched the Yankees take most of them, and I survived. I did not wilt at the first sign of poverty."

"You know nothing of poverty, Ellie. Poverty is not eating corn bread rather than biscuits because there is no flour to be had. Poverty is not having the corn bread at all."

"You think I'm a spoiled child."

"I think you are wonderful," he said, grazing her cheek with his hand. "But I also believe you offer more to Rosamond without me. The Negroes will come under the black codes, and things will be as they were. Not enough food in the cookhouse, no hoecakes for the workers, nothing. Is that what you would have?"

"That has nothing to do with my marrying you, Nathaniel!"

"It has everything to do with it. Do you think your father will be happy with such a marriage? When you might be mistress of a great house like Woodacre?"

"I do not think my father would make me choose."

"Then you are naïve. I'm not willing to take the chance with your future. Your father has made his opinions of my character well known. I'll not gamble with your life as well as my own."

"I'll marry a Yankee if need be, but I will not stay without you. The Negroes have been fending for themselves for a long time, and they can continue to do so. Once I'm married, there's nothing you or anyone else can do to undo it. Let it be on your conscience, Nathaniel! I won't do what's best for me. Nor will I live by your will or my father's. For once I'll do as I please."

Eleanor mounted her horse like a man, not caring for propriety's sake any longer. She kicked the horse and was off, blinded by her tears.

eleven

Eleanor bent low on her horse, racing alongside the Mississippi against its fierce current. The thunderous shelling began in her head again. Her mind brought back the fearful attack by the Yankee gunboat *Essex*. All the Yankees succeeded in doing that day was killing a young girl, Rosalie. How the town mourned her loss. Northerners invaded that day, and Natchez allowed it without protest.

Eleanor didn't plan to surrender so easily to her own battle. She would disappear from sight before she went back willingly. Something about Andrew was dark, yet no one would tell her what. Marrying him to find out his secret frightened her to no end. How could Nathaniel tell her not to marry his brother but not tell her why? It felt cruel.

The bustling port of Natchez came into view as she pushed her way through Water Street. The river was to her right; the great bluff to her left. She was officially Under-the-Hill without a chaperone. A rush of excitement pulsed through her. She slowed her horse and tried to appear nonchalant. But as she approached the wharves and warehouses, it was readily apparent a woman in riding clothes was not a typical sight along the rough-hewn streets.

Men shouted obscenities, showing their terribly boorish manners, but Eleanor held her chin high, ignoring them all. The sound of horses' hooves closed around her, and feeling surrounded, her confidence waned. She casually picked up her pace, heading toward the piers where countless ships were docking. Being without a chaperone suddenly didn't feel so freeing. She hoped to meet someone who might recognize her.

Surely there would be people of society there traveling—someone who might help her find her way on the pier.

The wooden structure jutted out from the banks of the river, hanging ominously over the water. Eleanor knew of the countless deaths associated with life on the river, but she took faith in the fact that she had survived the war.

In her blue merino gown with the white bodice, she suddenly felt improper with no hoop as she jumped from her horse. She held tightly to the reins, trying to ignore the eyes staring at her. A huge man, wearing an open cotton shirt that showed more than it hid, started toward her; and Eleanor straightened herself to appear taller than she was. Her effort was to no avail since the man still stood more than a full foot above her. His arms were so enormous that they looked like the flanks of a horse, and Eleanor gulped, preparing for his approach.

"Horses ain't allowed on the pier, Miss. They scare the livestock, not to mention the travelers. What's your business here?" He took her horse and tied it to a nearby pole.

"I'm looking for passage up the river." She unconsciously smoothed her skirt. "Are you in possession of a boat?"

The big man laughed but stopped when he realized she was serious. "Where's your lady's maid? You don't look like the type to be traveling alone. You running from home, little girl?"

"I am not a little girl. I'm looking for passage up the river. If you cannot help me, would you kindly point me in the right direction where I might purchase a ticket?"

"Missy, there ain't a flatboat or ship out there that will take you out of Natchez. Somebody's going to be looking for you, and we don't like questions down here at the docks. You just run back home before you cause any trouble."

Eleanor's heart pounded in protest. She had not come this far to be turned away. She didn't care how big this man was.

"I can pay you." She fingered the gold bracelet on her arm

and let the sun catch its sparkle. "This bracelet was my mother's, one of the only possessions left after the war. It's very expensive. I'm sure it would bring in a tidy sum."

The giant man came toward her. "Missy, this is a dangerous place for a woman alone. You just take your pretty mare and find your way back home."

She shook her head. "It's more dangerous for me there. I'm engaged to a man I fear is dangerous," she blurted out, pressing her fingers to her mouth. "Will you help me? I'll find a way to pay you if you're not interested in the bracelet, though I don't see why you wouldn't be."

The burly sailor laughed again, not mean-spirited, but jovial. "I think that fiancé of yours has reason to fear for himself. Looks like he found himself quite a stick of dynamite."

Eleanor crossed her arms. "I'm quite capable, Sir, much more so than I look. The home guard ran screaming before the Yankees pulled me from my home."

"I don't doubt it, Miss."

The big man tipped his hat, focusing behind her. "Nathaniel."

Eleanor turned to see Nathaniel waiting beside her.

"This a friend of yours?" the man asked, nodding toward her.

"You two know each other?" Eleanor asked, feeling as if she had been betrayed yet again. Just her luck on an entire dock to find a friend of Nathaniel's.

The two men smiled at each other.

"Jeremiah and I met yesterday," Nathaniel said.

"Well, run along now." Eleanor shooed him away with her hand.

"Ellie, I am not leaving you here alone. Jeremiah has work to do. Let's go."

"Why are you following me?" she demanded, grasping his shirt in her frustration. "You've made your intentions known, so leave me be! If you won't help me, I'm determined to help myself!" Her father would simply see her flight to freedom as an immediate need for her marriage, so there was no going back now.

"Did you think I'd just let you run to Natchez Under-the-Hill alone?" Nathaniel laughed. "Really, you must think better of me than that."

He grasped her waist and turned toward her negotiating partner. "This is my brother Andrew's fiancée. Jeremiah Coleman, may I present Miss Eleanor Senton."

"Nice to know you, Miss." The brawny gentleman tipped his hat again.

"A pleasure," Eleanor said flatly.

"She's quite pleasant when she gets her way," Nathaniel said.

Just then Eleanor had an idea that bubbled to her mouth without her giving it thought. "Mr. Coleman, could you take Nathaniel and me upriver? I'm sure my bracelet would allow for both of us, would it not?"

Jeremiah shook his head. "Miss Senton, as I told you before, I'm not taking anyone's fiancée away from town. Not to mention some high-falutin' daughter of a wealthy plantation owner. What Nathaniel does is his business, but I'm havin' no part in this scheme of yours."

She turned in desperation to Nathaniel. "Please, Nathaniel. This is our chance. Run with me and don't look back." She clutched his hands. "You'll have your dream of being a preacher, and I'll find some way to help the Negroes up North. Come with me."

Eleanor tugged on Nathaniel's hands, but the firmness in his stance dictated he was not moving.

Jeremiah did her a service by looking away and pretending not to overhear her pathetic attempts to woo a man into marriage. She peered into Nathaniel's eyes with tears streaming down her cheeks. "Please, Nathaniel," she murmured. "I'll be a good wife."

He pulled her closer by her waist, whispering in her ear. "I love you, Ellie. With all my heart I love you. That's why I need to take you back."

Eleanor felt as if her bones were crushed within her, but Nathaniel held her steady. She had allowed herself to believe freedom was within her reach. If only she'd found a sailor willing to take her bracelet, perhaps then Nathaniel might have asked the right questions and followed her. If only she had stolen away, maybe he would have come after her, and they would have been married quietly. Nathaniel's upright character was her stockade. No garrison or militia could save her now.

Ear-piercing screams broke her from her mission. It was a high-pitched squeal from a voice Eleanor knew. "That's Ceviche, Nathaniel! I know it. I'd recognize her voice anywhere. It came from that boat."

Nathaniel ran with her up the dock to a steamer ship that was forced low to the water with extra cargo. The screams were silenced as they approached.

A man stepped across the boat's entry with huge fists to his hips. "You want something?"

"I believe that's my Negro calling, and I want to see her," Nathaniel said.

Eleanor uttered a prayer that her instincts were correct, and they wouldn't both end up at the bottom of the Mississippi.

"That ain't your Negro. Negroes is free, or hasn't anybody told you?" the man said flatly. "You git on out of here before—"

"Before what?" Jeremiah appeared behind them, his huge stance as fearsome as the river itself.

"Now, Jeremiah, you got no business here. This is between me and the gentleman here."

"Let him see who's screaming. You didn't take her? You got nothing to worry about. It won't hold you up none, and you could be turned in if you don't let him on. You want the

Federals searching your boat?"

The man's face turned ashen, and he stepped aside. Jeremiah entered the plank only to be knocked on the head by the end of a rifle. He swayed but never lost his footing. He rubbed the back of his head, clearly steaming over the violence. He picked up the man as though he were just another bale of cotton and threw the flailing limbs into the river below.

Eleanor looked over the pier to see the man clinging tightly to the posts. "I can't swim," he called out.

Good, she thought.

But Jeremiah dove in and retrieved the man. The two of them came up on shore with Jeremiah holding the man by his collar. He met a Federal officer and handed the man over, wiping his hands of him before returning to the boat. Nathaniel had long since disappeared into the bowels of the steamer and come back up with Ceviche. Eleanor ran to her and comforted her sobs.

"They's got my babe."

"We'll find him, Ceviche. I promise," Eleanor said.

Looking into Ceviche's dark eyes filled with tears, Eleanor knew she couldn't just leave Rosamond. Without her, who would care for the former slaves? Her father would simply give in to Andrew's wishes, and the black codes would become a certainty. She looked to Nathaniel's knowing eyes. He had more wisdom than she possessed in her little finger.

A tiny wail was heard, and Eleanor saw Jeremiah running up the pier. It was baby Frederick wrapped in his worn blanket. Jeremiah held the infant away from his wet clothes and out toward his mother. Ceviche ran sobbing toward Jeremiah and cradled the baby to her cheek, thanking God aloud for taking care of her son. Eleanor could barely look at the young mother for the emotions it stirred within her.

Nathaniel towered over her, his muscular frame breathing hard from his rescue, which obviously involved some violence.

Eleanor stood and rubbed his rough cheek.

"You were right about going back," she admitted. "But then you knew that all along, didn't you?"

"I don't want to be right, Ellie." Nathaniel looked at her with the eyes of a man who by sheer will held her at arm's length. "You know that, don't you? I want to be your husband."

Eleanor nodded. "I know, Nathaniel."

"Will you trust me and not marry my brother?"

"How can I escape it?"

"I don't know, Ellie. But I know the Mississippi wouldn't have stopped you if I hadn't, so I just pray you're as resourceful with my brother."

Eleanor laughed, then gasped. "I forgot. I promised I'd be back for lunch."

Nathaniel took out a pocket watch. It was two o'clock. Nearly teatime. "They'll have a search party out for you."

"Yes," she agreed. "Whatever will I say?"

"Say you went after Ceviche. That ought to send a scare through somebody. Watch their eyes, Ellie."

"Will you come home with me?"

Nathaniel shook his head. "I don't want your reputation in question. Go home. I'll find out who took Ceviche."

"Will you see to it she gets home? And that she gets food?"

"Of course." Nathaniel set his jaw, forcing his gaze from her.

But she wouldn't leave him without saying her piece.

"No matter what happens, I love you, Nathaniel."

"Don't—"

"I should have followed you to California years ago. You would have had no choice but to marry me then."

He let out a short laugh. "You deserve so much better. I'm going to do what I can to ensure you have a husband worthy of your love, Ellie."

"So am I, Nathaniel. So am I," she announced before turning away with a single, coquettish look back.

twelve

"Eleanor!" Andrew rushed toward her, helping her from the saddle. Her fiancé didn't look the least bit winded, and the ice in his tea was still fresh. Yet his words were frantic. "Where have you been? We've got a rescue party out looking for you. When you didn't come back at lunch, we organized one right away!"

Eleanor searched Andrew's eyes and wondered if his fear stemmed from legitimate concern for her person or fear that she might be lost without their marriage to seal his future. Noticing his tea cakes on the veranda, his comfortable position didn't speak well of his true devotion.

"I'm fine," Eleanor answered, unable to remove her gaze from his picnic. "I just had a long day getting to know my horse. I shall name her Tiche. It's a nickname. Do you like it?"

She was certain Andrew would know Tiche was a shortened version of Ceviche. His eyes flickered in acknowledgement, but she couldn't read if there was guilt in them or not.

"Eleanor, it's a slave name," Andrew said quietly.

"There aren't any more slaves, Andrew. Remember?" She smiled and moved toward her cousin, who wore a concerned frown. "If you'll excuse me, Andrew, I haven't seen my cousin all day, and I must dress for dinner."

She hurried toward the house, its great columns beckoning to her. Looking back over her shoulder, she called out, "Thank you for the horse. She really is a beauty."

Eleanor raced up the grand staircase until her father's angry voice halted her last step to the landing. "Eleanor Sarah Senton. Stop right there!"

She turned, revealing her mud-stained gown. Its fine wool would never be the same. Shame washed over her at her father's rebuke.

"Is it your intention to ruin the reputation of this family?"

"No, Sir." She rubbed the cashmerelike fabric, certain its original softness would never come back.

"Is it your intention that our family name should be associated with Natchez Under-the-Hill?"

"No, Sir."

"Eleanor, you were seen Under-the-Hill today. Would you care to tell me why?"

She swallowed hard. If she had been seen in Nathaniel's arms, he might be sent away once and for all, and she would have little to say for her reputation.

"Yes, Father. I rode my new horse along the riverbank, and I ended up at the port."

"Eleanor, you are to be married in two days' time. I've given my consent for a quick marriage, which I think is best under the circumstances. I have let you run wild for far too long. It's time you began acting as mistress of a great home, the life you were meant to lead. The war has put things off long enough. Your mother would be disappointed if she knew you were still unmarried and running about like a schoolgirl. I pray she doesn't know of your escapades."

"Yes, Father." Eleanor curtsied, turning toward the top of the stairs.

"And, Eleanor—"

"Yes, Sir?" she asked over her shoulder.

"I'm glad you've returned."

Her heart raced as she fell onto the bed. If she had been spotted with Nathaniel, he would be sent away. At least until she was safely married. She eyed her maid suspiciously.

"Hattie, who saw me today Under-the-Hill?"

Although Hattie never left the house, she possessed a wealth of knowledge. Somehow anything that happened within twenty-five miles of Rosamond was transferred to her head without any sensible way of its getting there. Eleanor had never known Hattie to leave their property.

Hattie looked at Eleanor's cousin, Mary, before resting her eyes on her mistress. "I don't know, Miss."

Eleanor caught the stressed use of *Miss* and looked for some way to dismiss her cousin, to be alone with Hattie's secrets. "Mary, would you mind leaving me to dress? I'm a dreadful mess, and I am quite humbled by my appearance."

Mary sighed. "Very well; I'll go entertain Master Pemberton. I fear you were dreadfully rude to him after his generous gift, Ellie."

"I'd be most grateful if you would, Mary. Tell him I'm sorry, won't you?" Eleanor waited until the door was safely closed and glanced at Hattie. "What do you know? Who saw me Under-the-Hill?"

Hattie rearranged Eleanor's toilet on the vanity as though she had nothing of importance to say. It was just as she acted when a grand tidbit of information would escape her. "The new overseer went to meet with some shippers for the cotton. Word is you were on the docks with Master Pemberton."

"Did he tell my father that Nathaniel was with me?"

Hattie shook her head. "I don't think so. You have to understand Rosamond's people don't want you marrying that Andrew, Miss Ellie. I think they're secretly hoping that prodigal of yours might eventually win your father over. That new overseer will probably be looking for a job if you up and add Rosamond to Woodacre. Work isn't as easy to come by as it once was."

"Why did this new overseer tell my father anything, then?"

"He doesn't want you dead either, Miss Ellie. Under-the-Hill is no place for a lady. I'm sure you'll hear all about it from Mrs. Patterson later, so I'll save me some breaths. Why were you there with Master Pemberton? He proposing marriage again?"

"Hattie, how on earth do you know all this? That I was Under-the-Hill, I mean? Who told *you?*"

"Hattie has her ways," she answered mysteriously. "You weren't thinking of running off now, were you?"

Eleanor clutched her stomach, sickened by the knowledge that she was so transparent. "I love my father. I love Rosamond, but I also love Nathaniel. Every time I look into his eyes, I wonder how I will live without him. And I don't love Andrew."

"Don't go practicing for the theater on me. You got along fine for six years without that man; you'll be fine this time. Women have married for a lot less than love. At least Andrew has the means to keep you happy."

Eleanor stamped her foot childishly. "No, I won't be fine, Hattie, because now I'll be forced to look into Andrew's dull eyes. Eyes that lack Nathaniel's sparkle and a speech that's meant for me alone. His unspoken manner that tells me everything I must know without uttering a word. Would God give us such a gift and not allow me to open it?"

"I don't rightly know where God is in this mess, but I do know that your mama would not have liked to see you a spinster, and that's exactly what you'll be if you keep disappearing alone. A spinster or dead in the ground."

"My mother wanted me to marry Nathaniel, Hattie."

Hattie nodded. "Oh, your mother did love that boy. Every day he was allowed to break from his studies to play, she'd make sure there was sugarcane for him to eat. His father was so stern that he was never allowed to have sugar or popped corn. Your mother loved that boy as if he were hers. She always hoped. . .well, that's neither here nor there now. God doesn't want you to sin, Miss Ellie. I know that much. If you are engaged to Andrew Pemberton, the Bible says you are betrothed." Hattie stripped Eleanor of her gown and threw it into a heap on the floor. "Much as I hate to confess it."

Eleanor sank to the floor. "I cannot marry Andrew."

"You very well can, and you will. Your father says in two days' time—"

"Is that what you want for me, Hattie?" She crossed to the bed in her petticoat, throwing herself on the great mattress.

"Of course not, Miss Ellie. But what we want isn't always what's best for us."

A loud sound halted their conversation. "What was that?"

"It sounded like a shelling," Hattie said.

"But the war is over—what on earth?"

"You stay here. I'll check the balcony." Hattie opened the French doors and stepped boldly onto the portico. "It's Ceviche's man! He's gotten himself a rifle."

Eleanor stood, gripping the post on her bed. "What does he mean to do with it?"

Her pulse raced. Although it had been over thirty years ago, and before her time, the Confederacy had not forgotten the killing rampage of 1831.

"What does he mean to do?"

"He's pointing the gun at Andrew!" Hattie said. "He's speaking to him, but I cannot hear what he says."

Eleanor could not help herself. She made her way to the French doors, forgetting her half-dressed state. "Is anyone else with him?" she asked, worried for her family. "Where's Mary?"

"Miss Ellie, get back. You've got nothing but a petticoat on. Andrew's alone. Mary must not have left the home yet."

"Did Andrew take Ceviche? What is he saying to Andrew?"

"Shh!" Hattie warned. "Let me hear."

Eleanor whisked on her afternoon gown without care as to its appearance. The pagoda sleeves hung carelessly since she couldn't reach the buttons herself. "I must see if Father is all right."

"Miss Eleanor! You'll do no such thing."

"Button me up, Hattie. Now!"

Eleanor's tone left no room for argument, and her maid fastened her up. Without a hoop, the skirt sank dangerously low on the floor, but there was no time for formality. She rushed down the stairs, careful not to trip over the extensive fabric. Her father, Aunt Till, Mary, and the household staff crouched warily in the foyer.

"Get upstairs, Ellie!" Her father's voice boomed.

"I think I might be able to reason with Ceviche's man, Father."

"You've done enough."

"But, Father—"

"I lost your mother to the slaves. She gave her life for the ungrateful lot of them. Do you think I'd let you do the same? Get back upstairs now! Or you'll end up dead as your mother."

The angry scowl of hatred changed her father's entire face. He looked monstrous and bent on revenge. He held up a revolver, filling its last chamber.

"I said, get upstairs!"

Her father opened the double doors of cut glass and stepped outside.

Eleanor backed up, unable to believe the sights before her eyes were really happening. All she could do was pray. Pray that her father would return and this beast who dwelled within him would leave as suddenly as he came. She fell to her knees on the stair landing, lacking the strength to make it to her bedroom.

"Lord in heaven, bring peace upon this household. Please. I don't know what I'm doing wrong, Lord, but I shall humble myself to You now. I shall marry whomever You please. Only spare my father from this wrath—and Ceviche's husband, Lord. Help him run like the wind, and don't let him hurt anyone. He only wants to protect his family, Lord. Please help him. Help us all."

Another single shot peeled through the air, and silence followed. An eerie, beckoning silence. Eleanor ran to her balcony where Hattie crumpled to the floor, crying out. Stepping past her maid, Eleanor gasped at the sight. Lying limp on the ground was Ceviche's man. Behind him was Nathaniel on his horse with a smoking revolver in his hand.

"No!"

Eleanor's scream was heard, and Nathaniel peered up at her. He avoided her gaze and went to the dead man. Eleanor's heart broke for Ceviche, who had lost her baby's father.

"How could you, Nathaniel?" she muttered. "How could you kill a man who fought for his family?" The room went dark, and she remembered no more.

thirteen

The sun had set by the time Eleanor blinked back to life. In the darkness, she had forgotten why she had slept in the afternoon, but recognition came with a thunderous bolt. She sat upright, but her throbbing head willed her back onto her bed, and she groaned.

"Hattie?"

"Hattie's not here, Ellie." Mary came out of the shadows and pressed a cold towel to Eleanor's forehead. "She's seeing to your father. How are you?"

"My father—is he alive?"

"Of course he's alive. He's out at the slaves' quarters flushing out anyone he thinks may cause us further trouble. He hopes to instill the black codes immediately to gain control over the men. Heaven forbid this type of thing should ever happen again."

"What do you mean?"

"Nathaniel having to shoot that lunatic. Right on your front lawn. Why, it's just wicked that such a thing could happen in the broad daylight of such a beautiful afternoon." Mary dropped her nursing duties and took up her knitting needles again. "I'm telling you, Ellie—you are fortunate to marry a man such as Andrew. He tried to reason with the man, but he went on and on about his wife and baby. As though there's any legitimacy to that at all."

"Mary, what are you saying? I thought you were against the codes as I am."

"Only because I was ignorant—well, I shall not be fooled again. Andrew has your best interest at stake when he employs the codes. That should be obvious from today's treachery."

"What about Nathaniel? What did he do with Ceviche's husband?"

"I assume he threw the man in the river where the criminal belongs once and for all. Imagine threatening the owners of Woodacre and Rosamond and assuming he'd live through the siege."

"Maybe he didn't hope to live," Eleanor said defiantly. "Maybe he hoped to prove his wife and baby are not refuse to be carted off at Andrew's will."

"Andrew? Andrew hardly has anything to do with her disappearing. She was probably anxious for the chance to get away from here and thought she'd plan her escape. She might have stolen away were it not for Nathaniel who caught her red-handed on a cargo boat Under-the-Hill."

Eleanor rubbed her throbbing temples, hoping to will her nightmare away. But each time she opened her eyes, Mary sat calmly with her clanking needles, rattling on and on about Andrew's heroism.

"Where is Nathaniel?"

"I'm not certain, but his father was quite proud of his rescue today of Andrew. I daresay Nathaniel might get a bigger part of Woodacre after today. Should he want it, of course. Perhaps after his kill today he's thinking twice of becoming a preacher."

Eleanor could listen to the chatter no longer. "I must find Hattie."

"I told you, she's at the slaves' quarters, and, with your escapades of late, your father had best not find you out of the house. He's trying to prevent an uprising as we speak. Should a slave find you now, your life might be worth more to them if it was extinguished."

Mrs. Patterson entered Eleanor's room with a tray of tea. "Get back in bed, Eleanor. You need to be resting so you're not peaked for your wedding. Andrew told your father today's adventures only prove your immediate need of marriage. It's for your very protection now."

"Where is Hattie?" Eleanor asked again, hoping for a different answer from Mrs. Patterson.

"They're at the cookhouse now. Your father wants to see to it that the workers don't get ideas in their heads. Today was a very dangerous sign. It is a good thing Master Nathaniel happened upon the scene, or your fiancé might very well be dead."

"Instead, Ceviche's husband lies at the river. It is all my fault, Mrs. Patterson. All my fault. If I hadn't been so concerned about myself, so selfish in my thinking, Ceviche and her family might be together tonight."

"You're rambling on about nothing, Eleanor. Don't let your father hear such strange utterings. He already blames the slaves for your mother's death. It won't do you any good to take responsibility for something that is just a way of life."

"Is it a way of life, Mrs. Patterson? To be so uncaring and immoral toward human beings? Jesus said to love even the least of these. My mother did that, and I'm proud to be like her."

"And look where your mother is today."

"She's with Jesus," Eleanor said confidently. "I must speak with Nathaniel."

"Nathaniel is being honored at a family dinner tonight, Eleanor. He's a hero."

Eleanor couldn't imagine Nathaniel shooting a man in the back. It was so unlike him, so out of character; and it certainly didn't make him heroic. Had she brought such confusion by begging him to find a way for them to marry? Had this been his way to prove his loyalty to his father and hers? She prayed it wasn't so—that Nathaniel had his own reasons for shooting Ceviche's husband. Her stomach lurched vigorously each time she pictured young Ceviche with no father for her baby son. She relived the infant's desperate cries of the night she met him, his precious dark-as-coal eyes gazing wondrously at her and his calming sucking sounds as he nibbled at his fingers.

She had to find a way to help, but first she needed to escape her stifling room. Her cousin's interminable clicking needles and Mrs. Patterson's overbearing ways threatened to send her to the asylum if she didn't flee.

"Eleanor, where are you going?" Mrs. Patterson questioned as Mary's needles ceased.

"I'm going out for air. It's stifling in here." Eleanor opened her French doors and sucked in the chilled evening air. When the clicking resumed and Mrs. Patterson busied herself, Eleanor shut the doors quietly behind her.

Leaping over the veranda, she caught her boot in the trellis and worked her way to the lawn. Once on the expansive stretch of grass, she stole away into the heritage oaks and countless magnolias under the starry canopy.

A guard dog barked at her, but Eleanor calmed the beast with her soft voice and soon resumed her run. She ran past the cookhouse and into the stables. Peeking over the stalls, she spoke softly to Tiche. "Are you up for a ride, Girl? A pleasant ramble under the evening sky. We shall have a grand time." She spoke to calm herself as well as her new mare.

Only once had she been out this late into the night. It was the evening following the battle of the *Essex* against her city. She and the neighbors had promenaded to the levees to watch the great battle, never understanding that her beloved Confederate forces might fall victim to the Yankees. Numb, she and her compatriots returned home at a slow pace, no one speaking a word.

"Miss Ellie!" Hattie's firm voice jolted Eleanor from her solitude. She placed a palm over her heart.

"Oh, Hattie, you gave me such a scare. What are you doing out here?"

"The question is, Missy, what are you doing out of your room?"

"I wanted to see if Tiche was all right after the gunfire this afternoon. You never know how a horse will react to such circumstances."

She focused on patting the horse, afraid to look up for fear of getting caught in her lie. Hattie needed no such assistance, however. Eleanor's lies were few and far between, and without practice one did not become very accomplished.

"You need a saddle for that now, do you?" Hattie held a candle to her face.

"Are you going to bring me back to the house, Hattie? If you are, just say so."

"That all depends. Where do you think you are heading on this dangerous night?"

"I have to find Nathaniel, Hattie. I have to know why he shot that man. He knew what Ceviche meant to me. How could he do what he did for Andrew's life? Ceviche cradled her baby before Nathaniel. I need to know how he could take that infant's father so readily."

"I'll admit it's not the Master Nathaniel we've known. But one never knows what a prodigal might do to prove his worth."

"I just can't believe he'd kill for it. He would leave before he'd do that. So why didn't he, Hattie?"

"I don't know, but I expect you'd better find out." Hattie grabbed Eleanor's saddle and threw it over Tiche. "You stay off the path and listen for the sounds of anyone following you. And if your father or your aunt or Mrs. Patterson asks, I never saw you, you understand?"

"Oh, Hattie!" Eleanor raced into Hattie's wide-open arms and grasped her with all the strength she possessed. "Thank you."

"You come back into the cookhouse in the morning, and

I'll have a story concocted by then. You let me handle the fibs to your aunt and father. Your lying will only get us all into trouble. You are a terrible liar, Missy." Hattie laughed.

Eleanor smiled. "I'll see you in the morning." With a click of her tongue, she was off into the starry night. Her horse's *clip-clop* was softened as she trod through a soft, grassy field. She eased her mare away from the house before picking up her speed and pushing the horse to a full gallop.

Woodacre came into view. Candles lit the interior of the great brick house brightly. Eleanor dismounted, tying Tiche to a nearby magnolia, and hesitated a moment to formulate a plan. *Where might Nathaniel be?*

A hand suddenly gripped her mouth, and Eleanor tried to scream before hearing Nathaniel's gentle voice in her ear. "Ellie, it's Nathaniel. Shh! Shh!" He said, bringing her into his arms. She turned into him, allowing his warmth to calm her pounding heart.

"Nathaniel." She held her ear against his steady heartbeat, which inexplicably quickened. Neither of them uttered another word for a long stretch of the night. Together they held each other under the bright, full moon against a heritage magnolia, relishing their stolen time as if each star were placed for their view.

When Eleanor's eyes became heavy, she realized she must accomplish her task and finally found her voice. "Nathaniel, I need to know how you could have killed Ceviche's husband."

"I didn't kill him, Ellie. It wounds me that you would think so little of me."

Eleanor sat up. "I saw you, Nathaniel. I saw you with the smoking revolver."

"Faith is being sure of what you cannot see, Ellie. Do you think I mortally wounded that man? After I saw his baby crying out for its mother that very morning? Do you think I could be so callous as to rid that baby's father from our earth?"

"No, no, I do not. That's why I don't understand what I saw. I had to know what happened. Tell me and put my mind at ease."

Nathaniel unleashed her comb and ran his fingers gently through her hair. "Ceviche and her husband and little Frederick are on Jeremiah's boat to the North. Jeremiah has friends there who will find the family work."

"No, I saw his limp body."

"It's amazing how one can act when one's life depends upon it," Nathaniel explained.

"But I heard the shot!"

"A blank."

"They are alive?"

"More than alive, Ellie. They are truly free."

Eleanor sank into his chest. "Something I will never be."

"There's only one way I can protect you." Nathaniel continued to brush his fingers through her hair, and she delighted in his every touch.

"Not by going away."

"No, Ellie. By marrying you before it is too late. I cannot let your wedding to my brother take place. Perhaps I'm selfish or simply unwilling to sacrifice all of myself to the Lord, but I cannot let my brother have you as his wife. I cannot let another man touch you. I have no peace or rest thinking of such things. The Lord says it is better to marry than to burn with passion. I cannot burn this way while you marry another. It is not too late, Ellie, but by Saturday it might be."

Eleanor closed her eyes and played the song again and again in her head. Nathaniel had finally consented to marry her, and her giddiness knew no bounds. "We shall be poor?" she giggled.

"Most likely destitute."

"I shall wear muslin year-round?"

"There will not be a silk in sight."

"I shall say good night lying beside you each night?"

"That one thing is certain, my love." Nathaniel reached for her chin and pulled her into a kiss. Eleanor had never known such bliss.

fourteen

After a long night, sitting under the heritage magnolia, Eleanor forced herself away from Nathaniel's soothing voice and their lively conversation. She galloped toward home, where smoke billowed up from the cookhouse chimney. She smelled the delicious scent of bacon lingering in the moist, morning air. Her stomach's growl was hardly noticed, as her heart pounded for fear of what awaited her had she been discovered missing.

Samson, Hattie's nephew, waited outside the stables and took Tiche. He motioned for Eleanor to run, and run she did toward the delicious scent and her lady's maid. Hattie anxiously awaited her outside the cookhouse, her nervous foot tapping wildly. Dawn hadn't yet broken, and the cover of darkness shielded Eleanor from a deeper fear.

"Get upstairs," Hattie ordered. "Everyone's still asleep, and I made your excuses last night. You were under far too much trauma for an appearance at dinner," Hattie informed her.

It was not an untruth, and she would have little trouble corroborating Hattie's story. She had been too affected by yesterday's events to attend supper. Why, she was so affected that she wouldn't be able to appear at her own wedding on Saturday. The thought brought a smile to her lips.

Entering her room, Eleanor quickly inspected her gowns and climbed into one that Hattie had set out. She must decide which ones she could take with her to elope. The word sounded so sinful. She hated to think of starting her marriage with such a devious plan, but what hope did she have? If she didn't elope, she would marry Andrew. A man she didn't love, who felt it his perfect right to sell human beings. Even when

109

the law disallowed it, he had created his own laws under the black codes. The war and all its death taught Andrew nothing. Not even the loss of his arm had broken through his hardened pride.

Eleanor swept her arm across her vanity, pulling her silver comb set into the fabric folds of her skirt. She would have to sew her valuables under her hoop secretly after everyone was asleep. The idea soon struck her as ridiculous, and she poured her valuables back onto the walnut table with a clang. There would be no need for silver comb sets on the preaching circuit.

Hattie appeared momentarily after the noise. "Are you trying to wake the entire state of Mississippi?" She quickly shut the door behind her. "What are you up to?"

"I was just straightening my vanity." She reached out and placed her toilet in proper order.

"What did Nathaniel tell you? You did see him, I take it."

Eleanor nodded. "He didn't kill Ceviche's husband. They performed a play for Andrew and his father. Ceviche and her family are on a barge up North. A friend has found work for them."

"Oh, praise Jesus!" Hattie exclaimed.

"I'd appreciate it if you let the workers know he's not dead."

"I wouldn't dream of keeping such news from them."

"Hattie, I'm leaving." Eleanor looked into Hattie's intense brown eyes. "I'm running away and eloping with Nathaniel, and I can't leave without telling you how much I love you."

Hattie shook her head firmly. "You can't leave. Think what it will do to your father. He's already lost his wife. What will he think when you leave him too?"

"I hope he'll think he was wrong to force me into marrying Andrew," she answered, crossing her arms. "I have done everything my father has ever asked of me. Only now have I asked something of him, and he denies me. He will force me into a life of unhappiness if I stay."

"Have you asked him, Miss Ellie? Does your father know you wish to marry Nathaniel? Now that the man has returned, have you told your father you feel differently?"

"My father is not exactly one to discuss my feelings. I scarcely think he cares what the depths of emotions are."

"If you haven't asked your father, you cannot be sure of his answer. Running off with a man who's not your husband is sinful, and it will bring dishonor to this home. Is that what you want?"

"I cannot ask him. If I ask him, I risk Father finding out what Nathaniel and I are planning."

"He cannot force you to say 'I do' the day of your wedding, Miss Ellie. You forget you have more to say in this situation than you think. I'll not have you playing the victim. Your mother did not raise such a woman."

"Father will not leave Rosamond to Nathaniel. Without a marriage to Andrew, this plantation has a chance of treating its workers right. You have more to lose than anyone, Hattie. Do you want to see your nephew owned again? Your sisters?"

"Your mother saw to it that we were never treated as property," Hattie explained.

"And who will see to it when Father is frail? It certainly won't be Andrew."

"Ask your father, Miss Ellie. I'll not have you sin to make things right. God will not honor such a decision. Your mother taught me to read my Bible, Miss Ellie, and I do read it religiously."

Eleanor looked at the cashmere carpet that had escaped Yankee confiscation. Its design was intricately woven, and small replicas of the cross danced before her eyes. "I'll pray about it, but I'm confident in my decision. I love Nathaniel."

"It may take more than love if you defy your father. Don't forget that. I cannot support this, Miss Ellie. It's dishonest."

Anger raged within Eleanor's small frame. She wanted to please everyone, to continue working for the weakest as her mother had, but God seemed to be providing a choice. And it was a choice Eleanor didn't want to make. Her beloved, or her life's ambition. One or the other would perish in her decision.

Hattie quietly removed herself from the room, opening a Bible on Eleanor's dressing table. Eleanor approached it but feared what it might tell her, and she closed it without scanning a word. Voices mingled in the hallway, and it wasn't long before her door opened.

"Ellie? It's Mary. May I come in?"

Opening the door, she saw her cousin's tearstained face. "Mary, what is it?"

"I've been up all night sobbing." Mary still wore her nightdress, and her hands trembled. "What if something had happened to Andrew? I might have seen him die, shot before my very eyes. I cannot get the Negro's face out of my mind. There was so much hatred there. He would have killed Andrew. I know it by the sheer repulsion in his eyes."

Eleanor took her cousin's hands and spoke gently. "Mary, the man's wife and child were taken from him. Whether or not he had the right man, I do not know, but he thought Andrew sold her, and his anger was justified."

"How can you defend such a beast?" Mary shook her head rapidly. "When your fiancé might have been dead two days before your wedding. How could you be so unfeeling? Are there any womanly emotions inside you?"

Not for Andrew there weren't, that she would admit, but Eleanor didn't elaborate on her emotions. Mary thought poorly enough of her presently. "I am only trying to let you see *why* someone might have so much anger. If you could find who took Morgan from you, would you be content to go about your day the same way?"

"We are not discussing the civilized. We are talking about slaves."

Mary's expression held a frightening righteousness, and Eleanor realized her cousin had long been tainted by Confederate rhetoric. She had not the wiles to read both sides. Mary hated the Yankees for what they had done to Morgan, and slowly it had withered away her heart toward anything the Federals stood for.

"Family is family regardless of skin color." Eleanor spoke her view quietly and looked away so as not to punish Mary further. She fussed with her toilet and then bent over to splash her face with water and pat a towel on her face.

"You are not worthy of Andrew's love," Mary spat out the words, "if you can find any sympathy for that man—that man who might have killed Andrew. He's dead as he deserves to be."

"Thanks to Nathaniel." Eleanor couldn't help herself. She needed to point out to Andrew's greatest admirer that he was a coward, and nothing more. Nathaniel had followed Eleanor Under-the-Hill, ensuring no danger would come to her, while Andrew, her supposed betrothed, luxuriated over a tall iced tea.

Mary's eyes thinned. "Did *your* precious Nathaniel fight in the war? Did your Nathaniel ever do anything but rely on his daddy's reputation in Mississippi? How dare you marry a man on Saturday when your mouth betrays him this day! I repeat, dear cousin, you are not worthy of Andrew Pemberton."

Mary reached for the doorknob, but Eleanor stopped her with words that tumbled out angrily.

"And you are worthy, Mary? That's what you are hoping for, isn't it? That I shall give Andrew up for you? And you shall be mistress of Woodacre. You'd like that, wouldn't you? To fawn over my fiancé and remark endlessly on his medals and washed-up uniform that he wears ridiculously about town. How well suited you would be, spending a lifetime trying to make the South rise again."

"You traitor! You may have been born in Mississippi, but you are a Yankee through and through. I shall tell Andrew everything. You may pretend to be an insipid, sweet belle, but you harbor a heart that beats at zero. I pray no man finds himself wed to you, least of all Andrew!"

Mary slammed the door in such a violent manner that the entire house most likely awakened. Eleanor's feelings would be secret no longer.

Her breathing was rapid and strained. She fell against the back of the door and covered her face, sinking to the floor in a trembling, fearful cry. Mary and she were like sisters, but life had torn them apart just as the war of America had divided the states. Why had God made her so different? Most women would happily marry a plantation owner of any acreage in their postwar desperation. What was it about her that made her think she deserved anything more? She cried out to the Lord in her pain.

"Heavenly Father, do I sin to ask for love? The Bible says to flee from temptation, but where would I go, Father? If I stay here, my father will marry me off; but if I go, I will never be able to return. But how can I marry a man I do not love? One I do not even respect? Do You ask that I humble myself and deny everything I know to be true? Or will You honor my love and be with Nathaniel and me in our deception? Tell me, Lord. Please tell me."

Hattie pushed against the door and knocked Eleanor from the kneeling position. Looking at the closed Bible, Hattie shook her head. "You won't get any answers from God if you don't listen."

"Is Mary okay?" she asked timidly.

"She's locked herself in her room. I don't know what went on between you, but I can tell you she sounds as if she's packing to leave."

"She loves Andrew." Eleanor picked herself off the floor and sat down hard on her desk chair. "If she marries him, she'll punish every Negro in sight for Morgan's death and Andrew's near death."

"You cannot leave, Miss Ellie."

"I know, Hattie." Eleanor covered her face again. "I know."

fifteen

Nathaniel slammed his Bible shut. He had tried everything he could think of to deny that the seventh commandment applied to him, but coveting his neighbor's wife, his brother's wife, was exactly what he was guilty of. Engagements in the South were not mere formalities. They were a bond as serious as marriage. Yet he had given his word to Ellie, and since the Bible also cautioned to let your yea be yea, Nathaniel would run away with her and not look back. He would pay for it later, when he tried to find work or when he preached. Of that he had little doubt, but he would not let his reputation be ruined with her again.

He took out the latest map of the Mississippi and began to trace a possible route for them. Jeremiah would return the following day, and Nathaniel would discuss arrangements with him. Jeremiah wouldn't like taking Ellie out of Mississippi, but if she were Nathaniel's wife, he would have little choice.

The library door opened, and Nathaniel's father, looking haggard and blanched, leaned against the doorjamb. Nathaniel pondered how aged his father now appeared. Master Pemberton no longer stood an astounding six feet. His body had bent in the years Nathaniel roamed California, and the son couldn't help but pray his absence hadn't caused the hollow look that swept his father's expression.

"I was right about Andrew," his father said solemnly. "The slaves do want to kill him. If it weren't for you, he'd be dead by now."

A wave of guilt lapped Nathaniel, recalling how his one-act play struck fear in the heart of his father. "Andrew is not

116

giving the men enough to eat. We have so few workers left. Andrew shall be picking cotton himself before the year is out."

"That's why the codes are necessary, Son."

"The codes fix things now, but they won't fix things forever. You've got to think of Woodacre for longer than this generation, Father. Would you want Andrew's children to be destitute when the Federals seize our plantation for lack of complying with the law? Because that is what will eventually happen. The United States government will own this land if we don't submit to the authorities."

"You're talking nonsense now. Woodacre survived the war. How many plantations were cut into tiny farms, but we have prospered, and we will continue to do so." Master Pemberton stood tall, as proud as any peacock. "Yankees will never touch Woodacre. I'll die before I see that happen."

Nathaniel shook his head. "Father, I'm not trying to upset you. I'm only trying to give you another viewpoint. As someone who didn't witness the ugliness of war, I can testify to the Yankee stronghold Under-the-Hill."

"The Yankees have been here since 1862, Nathaniel. They haven't gotten us yet. Listen—enough of this nonsense. I came to speak with you about your future on this plantation."

Nathaniel shook his head. "Before you go on, you must know I've decided to leave. Andrew will be safe now that the attempt on his life was tried and failed. I'm glad I came home for a time, but I don't belong here."

His father hadn't heard a word he'd said. "I've decided to rewrite my last will and testament, Nathaniel. You are entitled to half of Woodacre again. Saving your brother's life yesterday proved to me that you are a changed man, and you are once again my true son. Of course, it is only right that when Andrew brings Eleanor home, she will be mistress of our plantation, but there shall be room for a wife of yours."

Nathaniel nearly laughed aloud. His father could give him

all the riches in the state of Mississippi, but the only treasure he wanted was Ellie. The one jewel his father saw as worthless was the single solitary desire of Nathaniel. Andrew could never appreciate her rare beauty or her marked intelligence. Andrew only desired her for Rosamond, and in his greed he had missed what was truly of value.

"I'm not staying, Father." Nathaniel neglected to add that he was taking the supposed mistress of Woodacre with him.

"I'll not give you another penny if you leave, Son."

"I know."

"I cannot give your rights back as first son. It is only fair that you should be under your brother's authority. Andrew deserves that much after losing his arm to fight for the South. Surely you wouldn't deny him that."

"I don't deny him anything." *Anything except a wife in Ellie, a woman Andrew could never appreciate anyway.* "I'm going to preach, Father. I want to tell the country how I've been forgiven and comfort those who have seen the wages of war."

Andrew appeared behind their father. "Please, dear brother, by all means go and spread the Word, and spare us your hypocrisy."

A chill spread down Nathaniel's spine. *Lord, help me to love my brother.* "I have changed, Andrew. I'm sorry you cannot see it."

"You have lost, Nathaniel. That's why you leave—because you know Eleanor would never marry a downtrodden, disinherited scalawag like you. Or should I say Ellie." Andrew smiled wickedly. "But don't worry, Brother. I shall take good care of her."

It took every ounce of self-control not to grab Andrew's neck and squeeze. Nathaniel closed his eyes in prayer, asking the Lord to fill him with the Spirit. When he opened his eyes, his brother looked like nothing more than a taunting weasel to

Nathaniel. His lack of appreciation for Ellie's discerning nature was exactly what would allow them to escape together.

"I am glad you took my advice and bought a cousin of Lady's for her." Nathaniel focused on the positive aspect of his brother. The only one he could conjure up.

Andrew laughed. "I found a horse that looked like Lady. I didn't go through much trouble. Matching up that old guard dog meal wasn't too difficult. Eleanor is not exactly a horse scholar, dear brother."

"I'm sad for you, Andrew. Ellie is a fine woman, and you are quite fortunate she consented to marry you. I had hoped you would treat her as such. Lady was with her for a long time. Poor Ellie."

Andrew licked his lips lecherously. "Now that cousin of hers, on the other hand—"

"Andrew!" Their father's horror at such words was readily apparent. "You shall not discuss your future wife in such a manner nor compare her to another woman. It's sinful, and you'll bring ruin upon this house with your lustful, coarse talk."

"I only meant—" Andrew was silenced by his father's remonstrance.

Nathaniel had had enough. "What happened to Ceviche?"

Andrew winced at the name. "Who?"

"The slave girl with the infant—Ceviche? Sammy's wife. Sammy, the one who tried to kill you yesterday."

"How on earth would I know what happened to a useless slave girl?"

"Because word Under-the-Hill is, you received payment to sell her. Is that true?"

Andrew looked to his father, then back to Nathaniel. "I'm not in the business of contraband. Is that why her lunatic man came after me yesterday? And died for his trouble?"

Nathaniel gritted his teeth, wanting to shout with all his

breath that Sammy wasn't dead. He was aboard a freighter to freedom on the Mississippi. "I'm just repeating what's being said Under-the-Hill."

"If you weren't hanging about in such a vile area, you'd know nothing of such lies."

"Both of you, stop it!" Their father reprimanded, clutching his chest. "Nathaniel, I am giving you half of Woodacre," he said through strained breaths. "You two must learn how to coexist peacefully on this land."

Andrew's face twisted at the pronouncement. "What do you mean?"

"Nathaniel is my son, Andrew. And as much as I'd like to reward you solely for your bravery for the Confederates, I cannot deny my first son his rightful inheritance. You shall receive the lion's share and final say, but Nathaniel and his wife will receive half of the plantation and live here as well."

"You must be toying with me, Father. Nathaniel and I could never share Woodacre. Why, he'll give the slaves beefsteak and potatoes for dinner each night. We'll be run into the ground before the first year is up. Is that what you would have happen? That this would become a freedman's camp? Because your soft son will turn it into an afternoon club for slaves."

"He proved his loyalty to me and this land yesterday when he shot that man. When he saved your life, Andrew."

Nathaniel swallowed the walnut-sized lump in his throat, knowing his father did not know the real story. He started to correct his father and tell Andrew that he didn't want the land when he realized Andrew did want it, that he desired it more than anything on earth. Including Ellie.

"I had a pistol on me. He just saw the villain before I did," Andrew said. "I am a Confederate captain. Clearly, I have far more experience than my cowardly brother."

Nathaniel started at a thought, before scrambling back to the map stretched across his father's desk. Scratched into the bottom of the map were the words "Corporal Andrew Pemberton" and the date "April 1865." Knowing the uprising had ended by then, Nathaniel mentally calculated that Andrew could not have become a captain as he had been portraying.

"Who was it that made you a captain?"

It was all Nathaniel would ask of him for now. He had more important things to think of, like how he would get Ellie tomorrow night and steal her away up the mighty Mississippi River. He would let Andrew explain things to his father.

"Excuse me," Nathaniel said, bashing shoulders with his brother as he exited the room.

Yet Andrew followed closely, pointing a pistol in Nathaniel's back as they made their way down the hallway. "Keep walking."

"Would you shoot me, Brother? Here in the hall of your father's home? When I saved your life yesterday?" Nathaniel smiled. "Don't worry, Andrew. I have no intention of staying and working Woodacre. You can put your pistol and your threats away."

The stabbing pain in his back dissipated as Andrew put away his gun. "I don't just want Woodacre—I want Rosamond. And by Saturday I'll have it."

Nathaniel tried to reason with his brother. "What will such greed accomplish, Andrew? What more could you want?"

"To prove to Father he has only one son who will bring glory to this household. And to rise up against the North once again with financial ways the Yankees will respect."

"You've done business with the Yankees through the whole war. Do you think I'm blind, Andrew?"

Pulling out his pistol again, Andrew traced his thumb along the intricate design of the firearm while twisting it playfully in his single hand.

"I have nothing against you, Nathaniel." Andrew looked

straight into Nathaniel's eyes. "Go out into the four corners of the earth and spread your religious babble—I send you out with my blessings—but relinquish your rights to Woodacre before you go."

Nathaniel stepped back and crossed his arms. "Very well, Andrew. I'll grant you that request, in writing. On one condition. Let Ellie go, and marry her cousin. Mary is the one you want anyway."

Leaving with Ellie would solve the immediate issue, but stealing her from her father and inheritance was not how Nathaniel preferred life to be.

"Mary," Andrew laughed. "Mary hasn't two coins to rub together. Why should I be saddled with a wife who has nothing to offer me when I can have Eleanor's fortune?"

"Andrew, I pray your heart isn't that dark. I pray you would see the need for love in your life. You were always Mother's favorite. How she cradled you until you were far too old for such snuggling."

The recollection brought tears to Nathaniel's eyes when he gazed into his brother's blank eyes. There seemed to be no emotion, no depth of life left. The war had left its mark on Andrew. No matter what lies Andrew told or what illegal dealings he was involved with, the fact was, he was not a child of God. And that broke Nathaniel's heart.

"Pray to your invisible God all you want, Nathaniel. In the meantime, I shall be rich and embracing the woman you love."

sixteen

"Father, I do not wish to marry Andrew," Eleanor said in her most solemn voice, careful not to show any depth of happiness. "I do not love him, nor do I think he will do what's best for Rosamond. I am asking that you support me in my sundering of the engagement." She lifted her chin, practicing a stern expression. She only hoped her father was as easily convinced as her mirror.

"Are you quite through talking to yourself?"

Hattie waited with her arms stretched out, holding a morning gown for Eleanor. It was a crimson merino and just the color to inspire all the strength she would need. Everything depended upon her ability to reach her father.

"I'm not talking to myself. I'm rehearsing. Aren't you the least bit anxious for me, Hattie?" She shook her hands to release the excess energy she possessed.

"I'm content in all circumstances. Your mother taught me that. She says I'll have a mansion built for me in heaven and walk on streets of gold, so I'm content with what He has for me here."

"Hattie, I don't know how you do that. I wish I had the presence of mind to be happy wherever God placed me." Eleanor smoothed on her white, kid leather gloves. "But I fear I shall not be content without Nathaniel, without something to call my own."

"You act as though contentment is a magic pill, but there's nothing to it, Miss Ellie. Sometimes having nothing is a blessing. I wait with wonder each day for the Lord and what He has. When I learned to read, I could be anyone on a moment's notice. I remember a quote I once read: 'The wealthy try to control their destinies only to be disappointed when they're rendered utterly useless against the wave of fate.' "

"You think my marrying Andrew is fate?" Eleanor removed her gloves again, wringing her hands.

"Now I didn't say that. I said it's in your best interest to be content if that's God's plan. I was born a slave, Miss Ellie. I've never been off this plantation except through the books your mama gave me. I saw your daddy grow up, and now I've seen you grow up." Hattie nodded her head with her eyes closed. "I'm content."

"Well, I'm not a victim, Hattie, and I'm not going to marry a man I don't love without a fight. And a harrowing one it shall be."

"Just a few short weeks ago, you were happy to marry Andrew. Nathaniel's appearance changed all that in a matter of two short weeks?"

Eleanor sighed. "It changed everything. It's one thing to marry when your future is without hope. It's quite another when the man you love stands in the witness box."

Three loud knocks rapped on the door.

"Here's your chance. I'm praying." Hattie fastened a lace collar in Eleanor's décolletage and stood beside her charge with hands at her side.

"Good morning, Father."

Master Senton walked toward the French doors with purpose, hands clasped tightly behind his back. "My sister and my niece tell me they are leaving before the wedding. When I ask them what such nonsense is about, they tell me I must speak to you. Do you have something you wish to speak to me about, Eleanor? Why are our relations leaving?"

Eleanor looked to Hattie and sucked in a deep breath. "Father, I don't wish to be married to Andrew, and Mary knows it."

Her father rubbed his gray beard and pursed his lips. "Is there a reason for such a decision the day before the wedding?"

"I didn't know you were going to move the wedding date up, and when you did, I realized how much I do not want to spend the rest of my days married to Master Andrew." Eleanor breathed deeply, trying to keep the emotion at bay. One crack in her consternation and her father would turn away from her hysterics.

"What would you wish to do with your days? Would you like to begin college? Or maybe you'd like to take over as the new overseer on Rosamond? Tell me, Eleanor—what is it you wish for?"

Eleanor cringed at her father's sarcasm. She did wish for an education and also the chance to see to the workers' needs to ensure a future under the Federal, republican government. But she was a woman, and, as such, she would ask for what was possible.

"I wish to marry Nathaniel." Eleanor tilted her chin high toward the delicately inlaid ceiling. "I wish to marry him and see him run Rosamond."

Her father burst into laughter. "Would you like to sleep on a star, my dear Ellie? Perhaps I can arrange for your mattress to be taken by sky train." But his laughter ceased upon her tears.

"I love Nathaniel, Father." Eleanor wiped her eyes with a handkerchief, angry with herself for her tears. The monogrammed letter "P" on the cloth sent a flurry of courage to her sickened heart. "Nothing will ever change that. Do you wish for me to marry the brother of the man I truly love? I tell you I cannot do it. I won't do it."

"I wish to do what's best for you, my dear. Young women are put under their father's care for a reason. Men are much more logical and more scholarly on such matters, while women tend to be of a softer nature, as God intended. Your mother's father ensured that I was a proper selection many years ago, and I shall do the same for you." Her father came close to her and patted her cheek. "I know it feels bleak, but you have had all the finest possessions in life. You have lived on Rosamond your entire life. Nathaniel became a different person when he lived as a nomad. Your troubles together would be endless. With Andrew, your life will change very little."

"Is that how one decides upon a spouse? By who will effect the least change in one's life? Hasn't the war changed me as well, Father?"

"I want you to apologize to your aunt and cousin. Mary is very distraught, and you shall never forgive yourself if she is not there to stand by you at your wedding."

"Mary will not come to my wedding, Father. Of that I am certain, and there will not be a wedding. You cannot force me to accept my vows. The words will not come, Father. I know they won't."

"You will do what you must to make sure Mary is there, standing beside the bride. A wedding on Rosamond without my sister and her daughter, our only living relations, would cause scandal and ruin. Now run along and apologize."

Eleanor took one final stand. "I love Nathaniel, Father. Andrew does not want me. He wants Rosamond."

"And who better to have it than a man who succeeded in the midst of a battle? While gunboats and cannons raged, Woodacre stood and prospered. The same shall be said for Rosamond. Together they shall be invincible."

Eleanor opened her mouth to speak but snapped it shut at her father's silent reprimand. Her arguments would only trouble her escape. Turning toward the door, she left her father with one last memory. "I love you, Father."

Eleanor prayed for the words to speak to her cousin. Making her way down the hallway, she stopped at a miniature of the grand portrait on the landing of her mother. There was a light in her mother's eyes that seemed to shine even in death. A knowledge and well of strength that went beyond the physical. It was as though her mother's image calmed, humbled, and prepared her to meet Mary again.

Mary loved Andrew. How was her cousin any different from Eleanor? It wasn't wise to love Nathaniel, and yet every bone in Eleanor's body yearned to go to him and leave her comforts behind. Did Mary feel the same for Andrew?

Eleanor tapped gently on her cousin's door and listened to the excited chatter that followed. The door crept open, and Mary stood in the tiny crevice between the doorjamb and the door. "I have nothing to say to you."

Eleanor stopped the door with her hand. "Mary, wait! I'm sorry. Please hear me out."

"What is it?"

"I apologize for my harsh words and bitter accusations against Andrew. I had no right."

"He loves you, Ellie. How can you be so cruel to a man who gave up everything to fight for you?"

"I am a selfish creature, Mary. It is not right that I marry Andrew, not when I don't love him as you do."

"You think I love him?" Mary tried to laugh.

"Don't you?"

Mary's cheeks blushed, and she paused before answering, "Yes, I believe I do. As sinful as I know it to be when he is betrothed to my very own cousin. And it is not the way I loved Morgan," she added quickly. "It is different somehow. I feel a kinship with Andrew because of all we've lost. You and Nathaniel have prospered over your misery, but Andrew and I have suffered greatly. It is not merely his arm that's wounded, but his heart most of all. Can't you appreciate that, Ellie?"

"I do appreciate Andrew, as I appreciate all Confederates, who so gallantly fought for the South and our way of life. I am not a Yankee, as you suppose—only a woman who sees both sides. I suppose that is strange for a woman of my little education."

"It is not strange—only proof that you did not suffer during the war. Your great love has come back to you because he fled. How I wish Morgan had done the same. But since he did not, I cannot help but feel Andrew's pain."

"You know I cannot marry him, Mary. It will be a life of misery for both of us."

"I do not see as you have any choice, and I do hope you'll learn to appreciate his sadness and take pity on him."

Eleanor pushed her way into Mary's room and motioned for the servants to leave. "Do you really hate the slaves, Mary? Do you blame them for Morgan's death?"

"Why shouldn't I?"

"Because they were pawns in the Federals' game, and we cannot spend our remaining days punishing them for it. It is not Christian."

"Why do you care what I think about the slaves?"

"Because when you marry Andrew, I want your promise you will not support him in the codes."

"Marry Andrew? Ellie, I think your fall from that horse did far more damage than we first suspected."

A pounding on the door interrupted them. "Miss Eleanor, Miss Mary, come here at once."

The two women looked at one another and hurried to the door. Mrs. Patterson's red cheeks popped in and out in the old woman's fatigue.

"What is it?" Eleanor asked.

"There's been an accident on the road. A young woman was thrown from her open carriage. She is not complaining, they say, but she is in and out of consciousness. Miss Mary, I'm going to move your things to Miss Ellie's rooms, and you girls shall share while this poor miss recovers. Your father has sent for the doctor."

Mary looked at Ellie, then at Mrs. Patterson. "Is there a reason she cannot stay downstairs for her infirmary? Why must she be brought up to the family quarters on the eve of a family wedding?"

"They say she is quite the beauty, Miss Mary. We are trying to protect her from male callers. She has an audience around her now, and I'm quite sure she will appreciate the privacy while she recovers. She appears quite distraught over the attentions."

"Well, how long will it be?" Mary asked.

"I cannot say, Miss Mary. They are being very careful in moving her. She may have broken her back."

"What about the wedding?"

"Why, it will go on as planned, Miss Mary. We shall just have to rearrange plans for our guests. Miss Ellie, I'd appreciate it if you'd help Miss Mary with her things. Hattie and I are preparing bedding for our patient."

"Of course, Mrs. Patterson." Eleanor bit her lip. *How on earth will I escape my quarters with Mary sleeping beside me? Only one day remains until my fate is sealed. Will a wounded stranger stand in the way of my future?*

seventeen

Sarah Jenkins grimaced in pain as her strong cousin lifted her up the stairs. She said nothing, but her expression said it all for her. Her blond hair, which extended to her ankles, fell loose and hit each stair as the two young people climbed up. Silence draped the foyer with shared melancholy.

"Doctor Hayes is coming up the drive now!" Mrs. Patterson exclaimed. "Miss Eleanor, you go meet him, and I'll see to the young lady's needs."

Eleanor ran across the summer porch, taking the steps two at a time, and met Doctor Hayes, taking his horse's reins. "She's upstairs. Mrs. Patterson will help you."

Doctor Hayes only nodded, then sprinted toward the house while Eleanor tied his horse to a low-hanging magnolia branch. She watched as the inhabitants of the entryway huddled around the doctor. Innocently, she took one step backward and then another, until she turned and broke into a hastened run. A run that led her to the stables and the freedom Tiche could provide her while everyone was busy. Eleanor's crimson merino hardly warranted riding clothes, but she placed a sidesaddle on her mare, coughing at the dust from the huge animal, and shimmied out of her hoop. She left it lying scandalously on the basin of Tiche's stall.

She mounted her horse and stole away quietly from the house for one last, leisurely ride along the magnolias before her possible elopement. Workers stared at her, but she avoided eye contact, not wanting to give herself away. A pleasant, morning ride, her smile told them, while her deep red gown belied another occasion: one more in tune with a morning breakfast on the veranda as a bride-to-be. The invalid had served a special purpose for Eleanor. It allowed her to avoid living the lie of preparing for a wedding, which she had no intention of seeing through to its conclusion.

Galloping to the end of Rosamond's long drive, Eleanor saw the crowd still lingering about the overturned black carriage. Its wheels spun in the air, and the sight reminded her how badly hurt the young woman must be. She involuntarily shivered thinking about the poor woman. Not far from the sight, a pink silk ribbon fluttered in the wind. Its length could only mean it must have been used as a garter. Eleanor jumped from her horse, placing the ribbon in the small pocket within the folds of her dress. She would return it to the young woman quietly.

Eleanor's movement caused the mingling men to turn around and stare at her. She nodded in acknowledgement, stepped on a tree stump, and mounted her horse once again. Making her way toward the path along the river, her arm began to ache, and she stopped to rest under a large oak tree at the top of the levee.

She rubbed the still-purple limb until the gallop of a single horse disturbed her quiet. Eleanor turned to see Andrew riding his buckskin mare, and her heart beat rapidly. She hoped he wouldn't question her. Hadn't Hattie said she was the worst liar in Mississippi? He wore his uniform as usual and a slight, cockeyed smile. Mary's recriminations haunted Eleanor, and she forced herself to take pity on Andrew.

"Good morning, Andrew."

"Good morning, Eleanor. Out for a morning jaunt?"

"Yes. And you?"

"I came to inspect the overturned carriage and what might be done to right it. Why aren't you at the house with the invalid as everyone else is?"

"There was so much confusion, and I feared I wouldn't get

another chance to ride Tiche—before my wedding, of course."

"Of course. How sad you will be to leave your childhood home, but how remarkable that you should live but a stone's throw from the great house."

Eleanor picked at the grass, looking wistfully at her childhood home. "Do you really think the plantations should be combined, Andrew?"

"They shall be after tomorrow, regardless of my thoughts." His crooked smile broadened.

"I don't think they should be. Paperwork could be drawn up to prevent it. I think the Federals may seize the properties and break them apart, leaving them smaller than they are now."

"You've been listening to too much gossip if you think that could happen."

"The taxes will go up, possibly to the point we cannot pay them. That's what happened to the Landers place. I read—"

"Eleanor, why would you worry your head over such things? Those are a man's worries."

"I am just the supplier of the inheritance, is that it?" Eleanor shielded her eyes from the sun.

Andrew raised his arm, and Eleanor flinched as though he might strike her. Upon sensing her fear, he grazed her cheek roughly with his hand. "Of course not, my darling."

Feeling as though he might press one of those painful kisses to her lips, she backed away.

She put her hands on her hips. "The black codes will ruin Rosamond. Our people will flee. They have been treated far too well to go to such inhumanity now."

"Was it humane for that slave to try to murder me in broad daylight? They are savages, Eleanor. They don't duel or fight as a proper man. They attack in the night like stray soldiers without enough to eat. The codes will ensure our safety."

"I won't let Rosamond go to the black codes, Andrew." Eleanor steeled herself against the tree. "I'd die before I let that happen. My mother fought her entire life to ensure our plantation treated its slaves with dignity."

"Your mother was a fool, and she died for her ignorance." Andrew's eyes widened. "Eleanor, I'm sorry. I was repeating Nathaniel's words. I should have known better."

Eleanor looked directly at Andrew. It was the first time she'd really looked into his coal black eyes and tried to find what Mary pitied about him. She couldn't see it. His eyes were dark, not just in color, but in emotion. They were as lifeless as the men in makeshift graves along the roadway.

"Nathaniel loved my mother, Andrew. He would never speak ill of her. Your own mother—well, never mind. It is wicked to say anything against the dead."

Mrs. Pemberton, their mother, was a callous woman who crouched over Andrew at every sniffle but denied Nathaniel's basic needs. Had it not been for favoritism by his father, Nathaniel might not have grown to a man at all. To hear her own mother spoken of as insane was blasphemy in light of his own mother's sins.

"Perhaps it's best we not discuss this now. On the eve of our wedding, we should be speaking of much happier things, such as the wedding trip I've planned. Would you like to hear of it?"

"No. Surprise me." Eleanor turned away from his empty eyes, torn between saving the slaves of Rosamond and saving herself from a life of misery. She hated that she was such a selfish creature and wouldn't give a moment's hesitation to the choice.

"Eleanor, I know we've had our differences, but it's time they came to an end. I shall run the plantations as I see fit. As for you, you may buy your furniture and turn Woodacre back into the showplace it once was. You may hire as many servants as you like and throw as many balls as our fair house can stand, but you really must leave the business to me."

"Andrew, I am asking you one final time to reconsider our marriage. What if you were to marry another and continue to build up Woodacre as you hope to? Two plantations will only be a headache to you."

"Your father will have no part in such a plan. Eleanor, you are just nervous. I know it has been difficult for you having my brother return before our wedding. I know that you fancy you once loved him, but I can assure you his appearance means nothing. I am offering you the future that any Southern woman would cherish. Do not miss the opportunity over a foolish dream."

"I only meant—"

"Enough. Eleanor, you will be at the wedding tomorrow as scheduled, or my brother will pay with his life."

He looked directly at her with his cold, empty eyes, and she had no doubt he would follow through on such threats if they gave him the opportunity. But they wouldn't. She and Nathaniel would run into the dark night before Andrew ever got the chance.

Eleanor shook her head. "Is that a threat, Andrew? Do you threaten me?"

"Do not misunderstand me. I mean you no harm. But I have worked long and hard to make a success of Woodacre, and I shall do the same for your family plantation. But I will not stand for this infatuation with my brother. It must come to an end. And it shall, one way or another."

"Andrew, you don't mean such vicious words. Take them back."

"Neither my father nor you has ever understood Nathaniel for who he really is. Now he comes back six years later, a walking ghost spouting his preacher babble so my father will forgive him. It's really inconceivable how he's found a way to break through my father's shell and be written into the will again. I do pray you're not falling for his excuses, Ellie. He wants Woodacre, and if he had his way, he'd have you too so that he might combine them as I plan to. Thank heavens, your father sees though him. Everything Nathaniel touches turns to poison. The ground will wither and die under his care."

"No, he doesn't want the plantations. He's leaving it all behind, Andrew. He told me so. He will preach." *With me at his side,* she added silently.

"He will not leave Woodacre, Eleanor. He will play on my father's sympathies and remain with us forever. He will live in our house and eat of our table until we put an end to it. But, as I said, it's not your worry. You'd best get back to the house and see to your invalid." He mounted his golden mare and clicked his tongue.

"Andrew, wait."

But his horse was galloping down the magnolia-lined drive. Eleanor dropped her face in her hands. After a few moments had passed, she took Tiche's reins and walked slowly back to the house. Mary stood on the porch, waving with a friendly smile, as though all were forgotten between them.

"Ellie, why, you're as cold as ice. Where have you been?" Mary took her hands. "Miss Jenkins is truly in pain, Ellie. She must lie on her stomach, propped up on her elbows. I'm afraid there's not much Doc Hayes can do for her."

"How is her cousin? The one who was traveling with her? Has he suffered much?"

Mary shook her head. "It doesn't appear so. He received a welt on his forehead, a great strawberry-colored thing, but he seems more concerned about Miss Jenkins than anything else."

"I shall visit her and welcome her. I have something of hers left at the accident site."

"She's been asking for you. It seems she feels terrible about troubling a young bride on the eve of her wedding. I'm sure you can set her mind at rest."

"The wedding should be postponed. How callous of us to celebrate while she lies in agony. She'll need her rest, and the music and merriment will only disturb her. I shall talk with Father presently."

"He has no intention of canceling the wedding, Ellie." Mary's green eyes darkened in a challenge. "He has already spoken of it to my mother. He is worried for your reputation."

"Why is it *you* wish for me to be married, Mary?"

"Because I wish for Andrew to be happy. That shall make him so."

"Only God can truly make him peaceful and happy, Mary."

Mary rolled her eyes. "You've been listening to Nathaniel and Hattie far too long. Save the sermons for Sundays, my dear cousin. You have hospitality to see to." Mary stepped away, allowing Eleanor to enter the great home.

Eleanor's father spoke in the study with Aunt Till. Their conversation seemed of the utmost importance, and Eleanor nodded in recognition while heading up the stairs, but her father called out to her. She entered the once-lavish sitting room and sat on an opulent, red velvet chair that now wore the knife wounds of a Yankee bayonet.

"Mary has updated me on Miss Jenkins's convalescence. I shall see if the young woman has further needs that only an equal might understand." Eleanor referred to the garter, knowing that if she had lost such a personal item, it would alarm her more than any pain until it was returned safely to her care.

Aunt Till cleared her throat. "The wedding shall be a quiet affair out of respect for Miss Jenkins. We shall hold the events outside on the front lawn so as not to disturb her any more than possible."

The wedding would be quieter than they imagined. For the bride would turn up missing as dawn broke.

eighteen

The sunny yellow curtains were drawn, and a somber ambiance filled the usually cheerful guest room. Miss Sarah Jenkins moaned in agony, and Eleanor nearly turned back for fear of upsetting the young invalid. A creaky floorboard gave the visitor away, and slowly Sarah turned around. The rumors were true, for she emanated beauty, even in ill health. Her cheeks were a fresh petal pink, and her luxurious blond hair fell about the floor, surrounding her like a halo.

"Good morning, Miss Jenkins. I am Eleanor Senton."

The young woman stretched out a hand. "Miss Senton. I am so dreadfully sorry to have interrupted your wedding festivities. Forgive me, please."

"Think nothing of such nonsense, Miss Jenkins. Your health is far more important. Is there anything I can get for you? Would you like tea?"

"No, thank you. My mother is being sent for, and they shall decide if I may be taken by ambulance to our home in Vicksburg."

"You mustn't trouble yourself. You shall stay as long as necessary to recoup." Eleanor found herself staring, for she had never seen such loveliness. "Where were you heading, Miss Jenkins?"

"My cousin was seeing me to Baton Rouge. My sister has settled there with her husband."

Eleanor reached into her pocket and brought out the pink silk ribbon she had found at the scene. She tucked it under the woman's hands without a word.

"Thank you," she said, letting out a deep sigh.

"If it is of any consequence, I heard the men speaking, and they said your fall was quite graceful. You did not show so much as a foot."

Miss Jenkins smiled, while closing her eyes in obvious relief. "It is of enormous consequence. Thank you, Miss Senton. Please do not waste more of your day here with me. You have a wedding to prepare for. But before you go, would you tell me about your fiancé? Is he handsome? What do you love most about him?"

Eleanor thought only of Nathaniel. "He is strikingly hand-some. He is tall with dark, wavy hair and green-gold eyes. They are the warmest of eyes and seem to dance with amuse-ment without his uttering a word. He is impossible not to love."

"Did he fight in the War between the States? Was he a hero?"

Eleanor's countenance fell. "No. No, he didn't."

"I'm sorry. My mind must be swimming. I thought I was told he was a captain."

"Yes, yes, of course he is. Forgive me—my head is not clear from the preparations."

"I should love to meet him when I'm feeling better."

"What about you, Miss Jenkins? Are you engaged, or do you have a beau?" Eleanor could simply imagine the throng of men who followed at the young woman's heels. Eleanor was thought quite attractive, but she felt like a toad beside this woman even in such a fragile state.

"I was engaged to be married before the war, but my fiancé died at Paducah in Forest's Calvary Department. He died a hero. It was a Confederate victory. It was a small battle, but it will have enormous consequences for me throughout my lifetime."

"You will marry another, though. Someday—"

"As far as the government is concerned, I was already mar-ried, and I am a widow. It seems Franklin took out a marriage license, and although we never had any type of ceremony, I shall be known as a widow."

Eleanor blinked. "What? What did you say about the marriage license?"

"It is a man's business. I am sure your fiancé has taken care of it, but it legally binds you before the wedding. The records clearly state you are married whether or not an actual ceremony took place. So I am a widow."

Eleanor searched the floor, breathing with difficulty.

"I'm sure your captain has acquired one, Miss Senton. Is that what rattles you so?"

"What would happen if your fiancé was found alive, Miss Jenkins? And you had married another after the license was drawn?"

Miss Jenkins twisted her face at the absurd question. "Why, I'd be guilty of bigamy, I would guess. Either that or I would not be considered married at all and living in—well, I shan't discuss such scandal, as we are ladies."

Eleanor clutched her chest, trying to gain control of her breathing. "Excuse me, Miss Jenkins. I shall return to check on you later."

Flying down the steps, Eleanor ran past her father's and aunt's concerned calls and out to the lawn. She had to find Nathaniel. Surely he would straighten this out. To her unparalleled relief, Nathaniel waited for her on the lawn, dressed for dinner. She struggled toward him with dread, as though her legs were caught in a quagmire. They buckled underneath her, and she battled to stay upright before she reached her destination.

"Nathaniel," she said breathlessly. "The marriage license. Has Andrew obtained a license?"

"That is what I came to tell you." Nathaniel's brow lowered. "I did not think my brother would obtain it before tomorrow, but it seems he has. He has shown it to me and threatened that if you were to leave now, you would be his wife forever."

"No," Eleanor shook her head. "No, Nathaniel. Tell me this is a nightmare, that we shall still run this very evening."

"I cannot take another man's wife, Ellie."

"You would take his fiancée! I fail to see the difference."

Nathaniel flinched. "The difference is our ability to be married legally. I'll have to find another way, Ellie. We cannot start our life in sin. I would rather see you married honorably to my brother than living with a scandalous title attached to your name. I love you far too much to let such a thing happen."

"But you will let him win, Nathaniel! How can you give me up so easily? He will ruin Rosamond, and me. Will you go on and preach without thinking of me again? You may escape a life of ruin, but I shall live it either way. I would rather live it with you."

"All is not lost, Ellie. I will find a way for us. If there is such a path, I will take it by the reins and steal you away as my bride. But I must do it honorably. I have brought far too much shame on my father to do this to him, or you."

"All is lost, Nathaniel. He shall have me tomorrow, just as he always planned. Why, oh, why did you stay gone so long?" Eleanor heard her father call from the veranda and lowered her voice. "Please do not forget me." Despair clutched at her breast. To be so close to her heart's desire only to have it ripped away was worse than cruel. The thought of Andrew's harsh kisses made her shudder.

"I'll do whatever I can."

Nathaniel's brown eyes spoke to her. His deep, jutted jaw left her breathless. She could not imagine life without him, and she wouldn't. Hattie said her father couldn't force her to say "I do," and suddenly she knew she would cut out her own tongue rather than mouth the words to a man who had threatened her beloved. Andrew possessed not an ounce of love or chivalry in his wretched heart, and Eleanor would not believe

God willed her to be married to such a man.

"Eleanor!" Her father's terse use of her name broke Nathaniel's warm look.

"Do not give up hope, Ellie. Pray without ceasing." He threw a leg over his horse. "Yah!"

Eleanor turned and made her way toward where her father stood on the veranda. "You cannot make me accept Andrew! You cannot!" She sprinted up the stairs and retreated in her bedroom.

Hattie waited for her with freshly baked cake and a warm pot of tea. "Eat something, Dear. You've lost all your coloring."

"I'm not hungry, Hattie. I shall starve myself."

"I've left your Bible open again, Miss Ellie. You call Hattie if you need anything."

"How do you stand it, Hattie? The feeling of being owned?"

Hattie laughed. "I guess I just think about my future. If we wallow in the pain, that's all there is."

After the older woman had left the room, Eleanor pushed away the tea cart and once again closed her Bible.

&

Nathaniel rode to Natchez Under-the-Hill with a pounding urgency. Riding up to the county clerk's office, he pulled his horse to a rough stop. "Whoa! Whoa!" Haphazardly, he tied up the horse, uttering a prayer Ellie would be there when he returned. In the cramped office a single clerk huddled over paperwork at a desk.

He stood immediately. "May I help you, good sir?"

"I need to see your records on Captain Andrew Pemberton. Apparently he's taken out a marriage license."

The clerk nodded. "I remember him. Missing an arm, right?"

"That's him. Do you have a copy of the record?"

"Who wants to know?"

"I am his brother and will be standing beside him for his

wedding. He stands to inherit a great deal of money upon this marriage."

The little man squeezed his eyes shut and then studied Nathaniel for a sense of honesty. "It's been filed already. I'm sorry."

"So it is legal." Nathaniel felt the life drain from him.

"As legal as it can be. I do my job with honor, dear sir."

"Of course you do." Nathaniel slammed his hand on the counter. "Thank you for your time."

"Enjoy the wedding," the man called after Nathaniel.

Oh, Lord, how will Ellie and I be together now? What is it You wish for me to learn? You tore apart a sea to save Your people from slavery, and I cannot believe You want Rosamond to hold Your people in bondage. And I hope You don't mean it for Ellie. Speak to me, Lord.

Nathaniel snaked his way down to the riverfront and noticed Jeremiah's boat docked at the central pier. He paid a stable master to take his horse and jogged down the craggy bluff toward the water's edge.

The air over the Mississippi was breezy and filled with the stench of steamers and their cargo. Nathaniel could see Jeremiah heaving great bales of hay onto his boat, and his stomach lurched at his predicament. He had planned to hide on that boat this very evening, sheltering Ellie, who would have been his bride, from her captors. They would sail away at the first sign of light. He had imagined it many times. Now nothing in his life was certain.

As he drew nearer, Jeremiah threw one last bundle onto his boat and stood up straight. His lumbering form was drenched from the physical labor, causing him to lift his shirttail to wipe away the beads of sweat. "Nathaniel. What brings you here, Brother?"

"Can we talk on the boat?" Nathaniel looked about him, and although he recognized no one, he trusted no one either.

formation at the docks paid good money.

"Come aboard." Stepping back, Jeremiah moved toward e bow and entered a small, private room used for steering e boat. Shutting the door behind them, he grabbed a tin pot om the stove. "You want some coffee?"

Nathaniel shook his head. "I came here because I need ur help, Jeremiah. Again."

"Are ya still plannin' on bein' here tonight? I can marry gally. You assure the future Mrs. Pemberton of that. I don't ant her frettin' about that."

"There's going to be no wedding, Jeremiah. At least not y own. Andrew has already secured a marriage license."

Jeremiah slammed the coffeepot down. "I knew your rother was no good."

"He's only doing what I should have done. He's thinking head, ensuring Ellie will belong to him. If I had been more orthright and forceful with her father, I would have thought to o the same thing. As it is, I'm paying for my lack of action. I oved slower than the sludge in a Mississippi puddle."

"So you just goin' to give up? Let 'im marry her?" Jeremiah cratched his head. "She seemed pretty desperate to avoid uch a weddin', offerin' me her bracelet and all."

"I know, Jeremiah. She is desperate, and I need to take are of her before she does something rash."

"What's more rash than running off with her groom's rother?"

"I'm not sure, but I know Ellie, and she'll do what feels ight if she's trapped."

Jeremiah laughed. "You sure God ain't doing you a favor y takin' that little spitfire off your hands?"

Thinking of her fiery spirit only brought joy to his heart nd a smile to his face. "I'm quite sure."

"All right, then. I'll help you. What is it you have in mind?"

nineteen

Hattie had come into the room and opened Eleanor's Bible again. *Hebrews.* Eleanor scanned it before closing it again. She didn't need a sermon. She needed God to act—and quickly. She still held hope that her hero would return for her and that he would overlook the troublesome marriage license. After all, Andrew would be as stuck as she was if he didn't cancel the license. Did Andrew hate Nathaniel enough to spend his life alone? To make them pay for her sins of leaving him at the altar? Eleanor couldn't answer such questions, and she supposed Nathaniel couldn't either.

Through her walls, she could hear the gentle moans of pain from Miss Jenkins, and Eleanor quickly entered the shared door to see if she could be of any assistance.

"Miss Jenkins?"

Quiet sobs emanated from the stricken woman, and when she peered at her visitor, her eyes were round and full from crying. "Did I disturb you, Miss Senton? I'm so very sorry."

"Hush, I'm just concerned about you. Is there anything I can do to ease your pain?" Eleanor took a cloth and dipped it in the washbasin, wringing it and placing it on the woman's blistering hot forehead. "You are so warm. You must have a fever."

"Call me Sarah, Miss Senton. I do feel dreadfully hot. I do hope I cool down so they don't cup and bleed me again with that butchering apparatus."

Eleanor winced at the notion. "You've had such a trying day. I wish I could give you something for the pain. I understand that tomorrow they will have an expert and a homeopathic

144

physician visit. Is that right?"

"You shouldn't even be thinking of me. You will marry your prince tomorrow. I hope the ambulance will come and take me away before the nuptials, and I shall not further trouble you."

"No, I won't marry my prince." Eleanor wanted to add that she would marry the toad, but she kept her animosity to herself. Her attitude was less than Christian. She chastised herself but still allowed the truth to come rolling out. "I shall marry the brother of my prince."

Sarah perched herself higher on her elbows and smiled, showing the first sign of light Eleanor had seen from her. "This is just the type of story to take my mind off the pain. Will you share with me? It sounds terribly exciting. Your words shall not leave my lips, if I should live to tell anyone."

Eleanor willingly told her long and detailed story, and Sarah listened with vigor. How nice it was to share the story with someone who wasn't tainted by the past. Sarah finally lowered herself back to bed. "I am exhausted by your life, Ellie, but Nathaniel sounds romantic beyond measure. I should be surprised if he does not rescue you. He does not sound like the type of man to leave you with your troubles, not anymore anyway."

"If he does not rescue me, I shall introduce you, Sarah. There is no sense for both of us to be unhappy, and I think Nathaniel would make the finest husband this side of the Mason-Dixon line."

Sarah laughed. "Ellie, he shall come for you, and I daresay any man would not be thrilled with the prospect of an injured wife. I shall perhaps remain a spinster forever." Sarah's eyelids appeared heavy, and it was obvious sleep was overcoming her. "Will you read to me from the Bible? I should like to listen to Scriptures as I fall asleep. My Bible is there on the nightstand."

Eleanor picked up the great, black Book and opened to

where Sarah had marked with a scarlet, silk ribbon. *Hebrews*. If she didn't know better, she would think Hattie had planned this. She read a few chapters before Sarah fell off to a peaceful sleep. Once in the chapter, however, she stopped at the words before her, and her heart pounded at the message.

"Marriage is honourable in all. . .adulterers God will judge. Let your conversation be without covetousness; and be content with such things as ye have: for he hath said, I will never leave thee, nor forsake thee."

Eleanor's breath left her at the searing admonition. She had complained without ceasing. She believed Nathaniel would save her, but he couldn't. Only God could save her from her lack of contentment; and until she made things right with Him, they could never be right within her heart. That is what Hattie had tried to tell her. She hurried to her own bedroom and found Hattie packing her trunk for the wedding trip.

"How is Miss Jenkins?"

"She is sleeping peacefully. Hattie, I believe I read what you wished me to. The Scripture, I mean, in Hebrews—was it about contentment?"

Hattie smiled. "I believe you read what God wished you to as I see your Bible is sitting there untouched."

Eleanor looked at the Bible and walked toward it. Her hand flew to her mouth with a gasp. "It is the same page."

"Don't act so surprised. God is mighty and willing if we draw near to Him."

"Everything points to the fact that I should marry Andrew. I can protect Rosamond, I can protect the slaves, and I can protect Nathaniel's life. But if I don't marry him all of those things will fall into his hands. Especially the black codes. Mother's wishes will be long forgotten."

"They already are being forgotten, Ellie. But you must allow God to work. He doesn't ask that you do everything by yourself—only that you rely on Him."

"There's only one reason to marry Nathaniel—for my own selfish desires. I must fight that, Hattie. Perhaps God's will is different for my life than what I had hoped. I must accept His will for my life."

"I knew God was working on you, Dear."

"I'll be at the heritage magnolia." It was her favorite place to pray. "Please tell anyone who's looking for me where I'll be. I won't leave shouting distance of the house."

"Very well, but you must be back to dress for dinner. We're expecting all of the Pembertons and a few neighbors as well."

"Is Nathaniel invited?"

"Yes, Ellie. He shall be here, according to his father and your aunt. God will give you the strength, Ellie, whatever you decide. I know He will."

❧

Eleanor dressed in her finest bare-shouldered silk for the preparation dinner. The soft pink color induced a rosy glow to her cheeks, and her fear slowly dissipated as she gazed at her reflection. She drew in a great breath. "If this is God's will, let it be."

Descending the staircase, she fingered the banister, taking in the details of the ornately carved balusters. Had she ever noticed there were pineapples carved into each base? As she reached the entryway, candlelight danced on the Italian marble, and she was mesmerized by the fiery reflective dance.

"Ellie?" Nathaniel's deep voice met her.

Looking up, she willed herself not to fall straight into his arms. Nathaniel never appeared finer. Clean-shaven for the occasion and dashing in his black suit of clothes, she marveled at what a handsome groom he would be. With his dark, wavy hair combed neatly, he smiled, showing elegant white teeth and an aristocratic carriage. The light of the candles shone a brilliant bronze into his hazel eyes, and Eleanor squeezed her eyes shut, willing herself to remember every detail of him this night.

I can't do this, Lord. I am not strong enough.

"Eleanor," Andrew stood before her, finally in something other than his Confederate uniform. He also wore a black suit.

"Good evening, Andrew."

"May I say you are a perfect vision this evening. Why, you shall have the entire town of Natchez hoping to marry you."

At this comment, Andrew looked callously toward Nathaniel, who hadn't taken his eyes from Ellie.

"Thank you, Andrew. You are most kind."

"I have taken the liberty of selecting a wedding gift for you." Andrew produced a long, velvet box. He opened it and inside lay an emerald necklace with dropped stones and gold encasing. Eleanor gasped at its beauty, but she instantly regretted her reaction when she saw Nathaniel turn from her. "It was my mother's. We buried it during the war so that my bride might have it."

Eleanor turned away from Andrew, and he placed the necklace around her neck. It suddenly felt like a shackle to her, and it took every ounce of strength not to rip it from her neck.

"It's beautiful, Andrew. Thank you."

He placed a harsh kiss on her cheek and whispered in her ear. "See, I can be quite agreeable." His breath upon her sent a shiver down her back.

A seven-course dinner and dull conversation dragged on until Eleanor could barely hide her impatience. She listened as Andrew told guests exploits of the war. Some new, some he had repeated endlessly. When the last guest left, Eleanor bid good night to her father and aunt and snuck quietly down the back stairs for some air. The cookhouse was alive and vigorously churning out smoke for tomorrow's festivities, and Eleanor used its light to find her way to an iron bench which decorated the garden. It wasn't long before Nathaniel joined her.

"I knew you would come."

"You look beautiful, Ellie. You shall make the most extraordinary bride. I wish I might be here to see it."

Any emotion ceased. Eleanor felt only numbness as she faced Nathaniel. "You are going then." She lifted her chin and played with the folds in her gown.

"Yes."

"I shall miss you, Nathaniel."

"And I, you. I've threatened my brother's life if he mistreats you, Ellie. He's given me his word he shall treat you as a queen."

"As he treated Ceviche."

"We don't know he had anything to do with that."

"No, that's right. We won't take the word of a slave girl over your upstanding brother."

"You're only making this more difficult."

Eleanor faced him for the last time. Powerless against his brother, she currently despised him for his weakness. No matter how strong he pretended to be by leaving her a reputable woman, she would remember him for his lack of courage. "I shall be fine, Nathaniel. I have reconciled myself to such a marriage. I was once very used to the idea until you came back and teased me. Do not worry. I shall make the most of my match and do what I can to help the people of Rosamond and Woodacre."

"One day you shall thank me for my sacrifice."

"I doubt that very much, Master Pemberton, but as I said, I shall be a good wife to your brother. It appears God is teaching me a lesson in contentment, and I shall learn it well. I am thankful we had this romantic tryst, that I might be the heroine in a Charlotte Brontë novel for a time and remember the days of my youth with folly. For two short weeks I was the belle of the ball."

"You will always be the belle, Ellie. Always." He bent down and brushed a kiss to her cheek.

twenty

Eleanor's ivory satin wedding gown with its wide skirt, worn over layers of petticoats and a full crinoline hoop glistened with elegance in the morning light. She fingered the handmade lace neckline, thinking such extravagance was wasted. Dressing had been a chore, beginning with the embroidered chemise, topped with a restricting corset, and finally the laced closing in the back of the bodice. She could barely breathe from all the layers, but she was thankful her wedding was in early November, rather than the stifling heat of summer.

She placed the floral motif Limerick veil atop her crown of auburn hair and sighed. "I shall forget Nathaniel was ever here. That is the Christian thing to do."

"Yes," Hattie agreed, though her mood had been less than Christian today. With every step she forced her foot to the ground, and when lacing up the wedding gown Eleanor thought she might die from the elder woman's aggressions. Although Hattie had preached to her endlessly on contentment, watching Ellie marry Andrew was like giving her own daughter up to a sworn enemy. Its toll upon Hattie grew obvious.

"Hattie, do not look at me in such a way. I am no traitor. If I don't marry him, we shall all suffer. I must marry someone, and it may as well be Andrew. I thought you told me you could be content in all circumstances."

"I can be, but I hoped for better for you, Ellie. I hoped you might find true love rather than settle for a life with Andrew Pemberton."

"I shall persuade him in regards to the workers. Give me time."

"You are far too generous with his nature. Your mother despised him as a child, and I think it was with good reason."

"My mother never despised anyone."

"True," Hattie said. "But if she was close to despising anyone it would be that strange boy who always had a snail in his pocket." They laughed together.

"All little boys like snails and frogs. It's quite a normal experience for boys."

"It was not normal to talk to them. And he talked to that snail just as I am talking to you this morning. Called it Rudolpho."

"Hattie, are you quite finished?"

"I am finished."

"Nathaniel is gone. There are no options left to me, and we shall soon depart for Woodacre to live, so I suggest you get used to respecting Andrew as master of our home and not bring up Rudolpho again."

Eleanor knew her tone was cool, that Hattie only had her best interest at heart. But the day was hard enough to endure. She needed Hattie on her side. A strange sense of calm had enveloped Eleanor. With Nathaniel gone, and no escape possible, she was determined to see God's will through to its rightful end.

Hattie's booming voice interjected, "As I said before, I'm content, and when I enter his home as a servant, I shall forever be silent."

A muffled cry emanated from the next room. "Excuse me, Hattie. That's Miss Jenkins. I need to check on her this morning."

"In your wedding finery?" Hattie asked.

"Unless you care to unlace me and start again." Eleanor laughed at Hattie's grimace. "I didn't think so. I shall return shortly for my bouquet, and we shall get on with this wedding."

Eleanor knocked quietly on the guest room door. "Sarah? Sarah, it's me, Ellie; may I come in?"

"Please, Ellie. Come in!" Sarah turned toward the door, still in her stomach-down position with her blond hair cascading about her elegantly. "Oh, Ellie! I have never seen a more beautiful bride. What a sight you make this morning. I was feeling so depressed until I got a glimpse of such beauty. My spirits are lifted now."

Eleanor twisted and turned to model her exquisite gown. "It is lovely, isn't it?"

"Not the gown, Ellie—you. Smile, Ellie—it is the only thing that's missing."

"I'm not sad, Sarah, really. I'm resigned. I'm resigned to getting married today, and I shall make the best of it because that's what the Lord would have me do."

"You are a better woman than I."

"How can you say such rubbish as you lie in agony and make nary a sound, Sarah? This gown would be twice as beautiful on you. Your golden hair is being talked of throughout the town. I've been asked if you might part with a few strands for a souvenir."

Sarah laughed. "Such folly. Men are naïve creatures, more vain than you or I."

"This gown would be beautiful on you," Eleanor repeated.

"Perhaps I shall get the chance to wear it someday if I'm not a certified cripple for my entire life. I fear no one would marry an invalid."

"You will recover, Sarah. I'm certain of it. Doc Hayes has called in the best specialists, and when you do you shall wear my gown and do it proper justice. I should like to see this gown worn by a bride who glows with happiness, as you certainly shall."

"Prince Charming did not come last night."

"No, and he won't be at the wedding. He has left Mississippi and my life forever."

"Such a pity. It was so romantic to think he might sweep

you away in the night and make you his bride, leaving his brother terrorized from the deception."

"It did make a romantic tale, didn't it?" Eleanor took a cloth and wrung it out in the basin.

"No! You shall ruin your satin. Your groom would not appreciate droplets of water on your gown."

"I can see you perspiring from here, Sarah. I cannot leave you like this."

"Call for my cousin. You are a bride today, not a nursemaid!"

"Pshaw! I cannot have a man standing over you. Your position is perilous enough as it is, and I know that would be my undoing to have a man see me in such form."

"We are too alike, dear Ellie. Vanity first!" Sarah giggled.

Eleanor's heart ached as she watched Sarah struggle with each movement, yet laugh through the pain. "I have nothing to complain about. I know that now. Nathaniel is a far-off dream. Andrew shall be my reality."

"Sometimes our second choices are truly better for us. God knows, Ellie, and He will care for you."

Eleanor nodded. "Doc Hayes has sent for a chair with wheels. Do you think you might be able to attend the wedding? I should feel so much better if you were there."

"Such a kind invitation, but I wouldn't dream of intruding on your day. You shall be the belle of the ball today, Ellie, not a foreign invalid who is more fit for a circus act than a witness to a wedding."

"Pray for me. It shall be a harrowing day. My cousin Mary shall watch every move I make all the while she cries at Andrew's vows."

"Mary has lost so much, and now this. Sometimes, life simply isn't fair."

"I know one thing. God provided your friendship for me, and I needed it to get through this day. To be able to tell someone, in all this finery, that I feel more like I'm attending a funeral than a wedding is such a great weight off my heart."

"If I am not here when you get back from your wedding trip, I shall write, Ellie."

Squeezing the cloth for one final sweep of perspiration, Eleanor kissed her new friend's forehead. "Wish me luck."

"All you'll need rests in Him."

Eleanor left and shut the door quietly. Mary met her in the hallway.

"Your dress is divine, just as we imagined. Won't Andrew be happy?"

"Won't he," Eleanor said flatly.

"I'm sorry for our misunderstanding, dear cousin. I should have never expressed my emotions for your future husband. Forgive me for such impropriety."

"You are forgiven, Mary. You were only doing what you thought was best. Trying to make me realize what a fine husband Andrew would make."

"I'm glad you've come to the realization. He is far too valuable to mishandle. Mitchell Rouse made that mistake."

"Mitchell? What did you say about Mitchell, my father's overseer? Or should I say former overseer?"

Mary's eyes grew wide. "Nothing. I said nothing about him. Only that he misunderstood Andrew's strength and saw his loss of an arm as a sign of weakness."

"How would you know, Mary? Mr. Rouse was dead before you and Aunt Till arrived."

"I've only heard things."

"What kind of things, Mary? Does this have anything to do with Ceviche or Sammy?"

"Oh, my, no. What would it have to do with a slave girl or her—" she stopped to clear her throat, "her husband."

"How did you know Sammy was her husband?"

"I—I just assumed."

"Mary Louisa Bastion, you tell me what you know. Or I

shall announce to the wedding party that I cannot marry such a black heart and tell the congregation of your love for my groom."

"Don't be ridiculous, Eleanor. You would do no such thing."

"Why wouldn't I? I have nothing to lose, or did you fail to notice that Nathaniel left for good last night? Don't pretend with me, dear cousin. I saw you on the veranda last night." Eleanor grabbed at her cousin's wrist when she tried to escape. "I know you know everything that took place between Nathaniel and me. You hoped for the opportunity to sweep in on Andrew, but he will not marry you, Mary. You are penniless, and Andrew's heart is as black as the bottom of an overloaded flatboat."

Mary looked straight into her eyes, testing her to see if she would follow through on her threats, and Eleanor held firm, never relinquishing the gaze. Mary soon backed down. "Very well. I shall tell you what I know, but only because it will have little bearing on your future now. Andrew has collected the marriage license. The only way you would be free from this marriage now is to ruin your good name, so I am confident my words will not harm Andrew in the least."

"Tell me what Andrew had to do with Ceviche."

Mary held her chin high. "He traded her for taxes on Woodacre. While your neighbors scrambled to stay as one plantation and not be divided, Andrew made a deal. He gave free cotton to the Yankees during the war. But only because he is a true Confederate and knew he would see the day when their money might enable him to spit in their faces. Ceviche had caught the eye of a young Yankee, and Andrew traded her for the right to be left alone by the Federal administration in Natchez."

"You seem to take an ill pleasure in that, Mary. Can you imagine being sold to a bidder who thought you beautiful?"

Eleanor looked into her cousin's darkened eyes. What had happened to her childhood playmate? "Does that give the man a right to own you?"

"Ceviche is a slave girl, Ellie. She's quite used to being sold."

"She grew up at Woodacre. She's no more used to it than you or I."

"It was shameful how you risked yourself to feed her. Andrew was right to be rid of her and now, thanks to Nathaniel, rid of her man too. We lost everything because of the slaves. When will your stupidity allow you to grasp that? That the South is no more because of slaves."

"The South is no more because we had more pride than gunpowder, Mary."

"Traitor!"

"And just for your information, Mary, Ceviche was not sold. Nathaniel rescued her and her husband who was supposedly shot before your very eyes. The family, including their precious son, moved North to freedom this week." Eleanor squared her shoulders. "If I cannot be free, I shall do all I can to ensure others can."

Mary's eyes thinned in rage. "I shall tell Andrew everything."

"Go ahead, Mary. You shall be gone when we return from our wedding trip, and it would be quite inappropriate for you to have an audience with a married man."

"You will stand before him and God, vowing to love him?"

"Have you left me any choice in the matter? When you think back on this day and how Andrew has been saddled with a great beast of a wife, I ask you to remember who put me there." Eleanor lifted her skirt defiantly, grabbing her bouquet from Hattie. "If you'll excuse me, I have a wedding to attend."

twenty-one

Eleanor had no intention of being a "great beast of a wife," but she could not resist the temptation to show Mary how meddling in another person's affairs would lead only to trouble. The guests milled about the lawns, and music filled the air. Eleanor's heartbeat intensified as the reality of her wedding finally took hold.

Looking out the second-story window, she saw Andrew shaking hands and meeting with guests. She had never seen him appear more social, and he had a smile for everyone. "Is that smile for me, Andrew? For capturing me, or because you have finally captured Rosamond?"

"It won't do you any good to be talking to yourself now, Miss Ellie." Hattie closed the shutters and whirled Eleanor around to check final appearances.

"I prayed diligently this morning, Hattie. God's will be done." Squaring her shoulders, she willed herself to believe the words.

"Everyone is getting into their places. Are you ready?" Hattie had tears in her eyes, but Eleanor forced herself not to fret.

She felt her thundering heart and drew in a thorough, cleansing breath. "I am as ready as I'll ever be."

The wedding march began, and Eleanor met her father at the stair landing. "You look lovely, Eleanor. So much like your mother on her wedding day. She was queen of the court. I have never seen another bride that held a candle to her. Until today."

Eleanor smiled and squeezed her father's hand. "I am sorry

I've been so defiant, Father. About Nathaniel and the rest."

"Never mind. It is all finished now. A woman's heart gives itself so rarely. I just have to remember how young you were when he charmed you. But Andrew shall make a good husband, Ellie, and a good owner for Rosamond."

Eleanor nodded, unable to speak, for she still thought Andrew would make a terrible overseer of Rosamond. Perhaps her father was right, though. What did a woman know of such matters? Eleanor's heart was always swayed by the plight of the slaves, just as her mother's heart had been. Yet her mother still loved and respected her father, and she would learn to do the same for Andrew.

The wedding march began again, and Eleanor descended the final stair, turning toward her father. "I wish Mother were here."

"If she hadn't nursed those slaves with the fever, she would be." Her father must have realized his harshness, for he squeezed her hand and looked into her eyes. "Your mother's soft nature got the best of her, Ellie. That is why I wish for you to marry Andrew. I know he will not let your kindly nature kill you. If only I'd put my foot down," Master Senton said, lowering his head, "she would be here with us now, watching her daughter get married. My weakness killed your mother."

Eleanor shook her head. "Oh, no, Father. Mother died the way she lived, loving others. *Andrew,*" she couldn't help herself; she spat his name, "Andrew, may well remember her as a fool for her kindness, but I shall always know her as one who gave herself up for others. There is no higher calling than that, Father. Mother would not wish it any other way." Finally, Eleanor understood why her father was so adamant about Andrew as a husband.

As the wedding march trickled into their conversation, Eleanor wrapped her arms around her father, and his tight, answering hug gave her the strength she would need to follow through with this wedding mockery.

Starting down the makeshift aisle between garden seats, she saw Andrew standing at the end of the altar beside Preacher Cummings, dressed in black. Eleanor wished her own dress might match her mood. Andrew smiled his crooked smile, as if to tell her he had won. She needed no reminder. Reaching her place before the preacher, she could not look at her groom. His gloating was too much for her wearied heart.

The roar of horses overpowered the preacher's introductions, and Eleanor looked up to see several Federal officers in full dress. A colonel jumped from his horse, and the others followed. They approached the young couple with resolute steps.

"Master Andrew Pemberton?"

Stepping back in fear, Eleanor answered for him. "This is Master Pemberton."

"You are under arrest for impersonating an officer."

Eleanor's knees were suddenly weak, and she giggled nervously, catching her inappropriate action and covering her mouth. "Under arrest?" She bit her lip to force back the relief that bubbled within her. "Is there some mistake?" How she hoped there was not. Her heart beat faster with hope, and she turned to see Andrew's face blanched with his shock.

"No mistake, Miss. We are sorry to have selected such an inopportune time, but it has come to our attention that your groom has been impersonating a Confederate captain. He has signed federal documents regarding your marriage with a false title. He is under arrest for impersonating a captain and submitting false documents to the federal government."

Mary shrieked and nearly swooned but was caught by her mother who fanned her daughter, pulling her back to a standing position. As Andrew was being escorted away, Mary grasped at his arm, and he returned her look.

"Nathaniel is behind this!" Andrew exclaimed, before turning on his heel and running from his captors.

"Andrew, no!" Mary screamed.

"Halt!" The Union officer readied his gun while a collective gasp went up in the gathering. But Andrew was far too much of a coward to be shot, and he stopped immediately, holding up his head proudly as the Federals reached him.

Andrew looked at his jilted bride. "I shall return when this is sorted out, and I shall have you as my wife. You, and Rosamond."

"I shall wait for you, Andrew!" Mary called, waving her lace handkerchief.

Eleanor stepped to Andrew's side and whispered in his ear: "I *shan't* wait for you. A criminal and a coward will *never* own Rosamond!" A wash of betrayal came over her, as she recalled how Andrew had accused Nathaniel of such evil, while portraying the perfect brother and son. The sense of release nearly made her giddy. Free. She was free of his suffocating determination.

Andrew's eyes thinned in his loathing of her, challenging her that all was not lost, that he would be back. She turned away, certain her father would never trust him again. Eleanor's heart warmed to memories of Nathaniel. While he may have left, his legacy lingered. He had saved her from a perilous life. For that and so much more, she would always love him. No other man would ever have her, save the man who had turned his own brother over to the law, rather than risk her married to a man who despised her.

She threw off her veil and faced her friends, trying to feign disappointment and humiliation. "There shall be no wedding today. I'm dreadfully sorry you have witnessed my fiancé on his way to jail."

"May you rot for this, Eleanor!" Mary nearly jumped on

her but was held back by her mother's lumbering frame.

"Mary! Control yourself this instant!"

Eleanor stepped to her father's side. "I'm sorry I have let you down, Father."

He stared at the rich earth. "You have not let me down, Eleanor. I cannot believe Andrew did not earn the rank of captain."

"He is unscrupulous, Father. He fooled us all."

The sound of hooves alerted them to another rider's arrival, and Eleanor saw at once that it was Nathaniel. She felt her breathing stop. She closed her eyes and pinched herself. Opening them several times, she finally convinced herself he was no apparition. She ran toward him without thought to propriety or her bouncing hoop, only her trail of satin and lace. His full smile reached her, and she called out his name as she drew near. Jumping from his horse, he took her into his arms and embraced her with such strength she thought he might never let her go. His heart pounded against her ear, and she returned his embrace with all her might.

"What is the meaning of this?" Her father came beside them, looking back to the awestruck audience. "I demand you remove your hands from my daughter this instant! She shall have nothing to do with a Pemberton from here on out."

"I'm afraid she has little choice." Nathaniel took out a piece of paper from his pocket and shook it out, handing it to her father. "I have obtained a marriage license in our names, and I am sorry, Sir, but I shall not release her. She shall be my bride or nobody's."

"This is blackmail." Master Senton's eyes narrowed. "Didn't your father raise a proper Southern gentleman? You shall not own Rosamond, if that's what you are thinking."

"I shan't care. It is not Rosamond I want."

Nathaniel looked down upon her, his gold-flecked eyes sparkling above his smile. Although her father was standing beside them, they were never more alone, for his intimate gaze spoke only to her.

"I should never have doubted you, Nathaniel."

"I lost you once, Ellie. I am not shallow enough to do it twice."

"They'll not hang him, will they?"

"No. If he had impersonated a Federal officer, they would have. But as it is, they are more concerned about his taking out a government marriage license, which would have caused them to falsify documents. He made them out to be fools, and the Union is far too concerned about reconstruction to let that happen."

"That was quite clever," her father interjected, his eyes still narrowed. "But tell me why you would go through such trouble if it is not Rosamond you want?"

Nathaniel gazed upon Ellie before turning to Master Senton. "How can you possibly question me, Sir? Which is more valuable to you, Rosamond or Ellie? To what lengths would you go?"

Her father dropped his head into his hands. "The ends of the earth, Nathaniel. The ends of the earth."

"As will I, Sir. I love your daughter. I know I am not what you would dream of for a son, but is my brother? His true image was cast behind smoke, and he never truly valued your family or Ellie. I shall value her with my whole being with the Lord's help."

Her father still did not appear convinced. "Andrew valued the South and tradition. He would not allow Ellie's emotions to get the better of her."

"She would have no emotions if she married him. They would all fail her to avoid the misery he would have placed her in. Is that what you wish for her?"

Her father looked at her with a tear glistening in his eye. "I thought that's what I wished for her, but she is so like her mother. I should say that asking Ellie to stop feeling for others is asking her to die."

"Precisely."

"Her life is what I tried to protect."

"I shall protect it. With all that is in me. Leave Rosamond to whomever you deem fit—it makes no difference to me, so long as I spend my days with Eleanor. We shall live on the North Sixty my father has willed to me, in a tiny cabin. We shall not be there for long. Ellie deserves to live as a queen, and I will make it so, but it may not be the way you seek. I have spent far too long searching for riches, only to discover the Lord's grace is worth more than any earthly fortune. I am home now. Home to stay, and I have never been wealthier." His arm came around Ellie, and he squeezed her tight.

"Do you mean to state you will not release my daughter from this marriage certificate you have unlawfully acquired?" Master Senton frowned, but Eleanor saw the light in his eye.

"I do," Nathaniel said.

"Then we may as well take advantage of the preacher's presence," Master Senton said.

"Daddy, really?" Eleanor looked at her father, who hid his smile. She embraced him, releasing tender kisses all over his face. "You are a romantic, Father. Just as Mother always claimed you to be!"

"You are all I have left of her, Ellie. To think I almost killed my own little girl trying to protect her from her true fate. To see your light extinguished would most certainly mean the death of the true Ellie. Go and marry your prince, but remember me as wanting only the best for you."

"Another opinion never crossed my mind," Eleanor said.

He cleared his throat and turned to her groom. "You shall have Rosamond, Nathaniel. You are a true prodigal, worthy of the inheritance."

Master Senton shook hands with Nathaniel, and Eleanor

grasped their handshake, smiling for the world to see.

"We must tell our friends before they all leave, Father."

"Let them go. They will only talk."

"Let them talk, but they shall never witness another wedding where the groom loves his bride more," Nathaniel said.

"It is bad luck to see the bride before the wedding!" Eleanor suddenly exclaimed.

"No, Ellie. I have brought the bad luck upon you, and I shall be certain it ends." Master Senton kissed the top of her head.

"I must grab my veil. Father, meet me in the foyer, and we shall start this day again!" She sprinted toward the house, picking up her veil on the way. "There is to be a wedding today!"

Her unabashed smile caused a rush of nervous laughter through the small crowd. All except her aunt and Mary, who stood with crossed arms waiting for her father, ready to offer him a piece of their minds. *Well, let them complain,* she thought. *Father shall not listen today.*

Joyfully, she skipped to the house.

twenty-two

"Sarah! Sarah!" Eleanor burst through the guest room door to find her friend biting her lip in pain. "Oh, dear Sarah, you are miserable today. Aren't you?"

Sarah shook her head and smiled. "Tell me your happy news. Has he come for you?"

"He has. Andrew has been sent to jail. He was never a Confederate captain."

"I do not wish to hear of *him*," Sarah answered. "Tell me about Nathaniel. Will you marry him?"

"He has obtained a marriage license. According to the government, I belong officially to Nathaniel. The marriage ceremony is a mere formality, but one I shall readily welcome. Will you come down, Sarah? It is to be in a few moments. As soon as they pull the preacher off the floor from his shock," she said, giggling.

"Ellie, how I would love to, but I fear I cannot sit up in my chair. Doctor Hayes thinks I may have broken my spine. My cousin tried to move me today, and it was not successful. But I shall have him move my bed to the window and watch from here. Would that be all right?"

Eleanor's shoulders slumped. "I wish you could be there, Sarah. It shall not be the same without you and with my cousin Mary looking over my shoulder."

"Ellie, don't say such things. Mary cannot help herself. She has seen so much grief in her short lifetime. Something about Andrew touches her. Who are we to judge?"

"Of course, you are right. As much as I resent it. Nothing shall steal my joy today. Shame on me for allowing it to."

"The next time I see you it shall be as a married woman. Oh, I do hope you won't find me here upon your return."

"I do as well, Sarah—only because I want you to run down our staircase in victory." Eleanor bent and kissed her beloved new friend. "I shall wave from below."

"Good-bye, dear Ellie."

Eleanor bounded down the stairs and greeted her waiting father.

"Are we ready?"

"I can hardly wait!"

Looking outdoors, Eleanor spotted Nathaniel. His dark, wavy locks blew in the slight breeze of the unseasonably warm day. He smiled to all around him, shaking hands and nodding his head. The joy in his eyes could not be denied, and Eleanor wondered what she had done to deserve a life with this man.

He had left a mere boy with unrealistic dreams and lofty goals but come back a welcomed prodigal. A spiritually mature man, who finally loved the Lord more than himself. Eleanor watched him with awe. How his leaving had changed him, and how she had prayed he wouldn't run to California. But if he hadn't, her handsome prodigal wouldn't be standing here this moment. Ready to marry her and cherish her always. How unlike the spoiled child who left.

She drew in a deep breath and looked at her father. "This day is better than I possibly imagined it. God takes our dreams and multiplies them."

Her father kissed her cheek. "I was thinking exactly the same thing. I know if your mother could be here, she would have tears in her eyes watching you walk this aisle. Only a few short moments ago, I was ready to give you away to a man I knew didn't love you properly but who I felt would take care of you. Now I give you with my blessings, with no reservations, Ellie."

"I am so glad, Father. Aunt Till still thinks Andrew is the better Pemberton, doesn't she?" Eleanor wished her aunt and cousin saw Andrew for who he truly was, but she couldn't let their lack of support steal her joy.

"He will probably still inherit the lion's share of Woodacre. To your aunt, who lost everything in the war, that means stability." He squeezed her hand. "Wouldn't we all wish to stand on solid rock if given a choice?"

"There is only One, though."

"How true, Ellie. I think I forgot that for awhile. You have grown to be such a fine young woman." He brushed her cheek. "Your mother's efforts, though short, have paid off. You have her beauty and her heart. But it is time I must part with you, for Nathaniel seems to be pacing nervously like a wild cat."

Eleanor giggled. "I cannot believe I am ready to marry him."

"Here we go."

The wedding march began for a third time, and Eleanor's stomach fluttered with excitement. Her gown trailed magnificently behind her, and she felt Hattie tug at it, so it would lie just right. Straightening her veil, she moved toward Nathaniel as though pulled by an unseen force. She was certain an ample audience still remained to witness the strange proceedings, but she couldn't name a single person. For her eyes never left him. His squared jaw and regal facial structure remained solemn until she reached him. Then he looked upon her with a smile colored by heaven above.

He held her hands and repeated the preacher's words.

"I take thee, Eleanor, to be my lawfully wedded wife. To have and to hold."

His whispered words seemed only for her and the Lord. She blissfully wrapped her memory around each syllable, storing it for future use. She would remember always the warm expression on his face, the sparkle in his eyes, the warmth from his hands.

"I take thee, Nathaniel, to be my lawfully wedded husband."

The ring ceremony was next, and Eleanor's eyes widened. *Do you have a ring?* her expression asked. But without hesitation Jeremiah, Nathaniel's best man, pulled a gem from his pocket.

Rather than the simple gold band Eleanor expected from her pauper groom, Nathaniel held out a gold filigree crown-shaped ring, which held an elegant emerald, but in a brilliant green circle.

She couldn't help her thoughts from tumbling out. "Where did you get this?"

"It was the one thing I brought back with me from California." He slipped the gorgeous ring onto her finger. "You are the only reason I returned."

Eleanor wiped away a tear and sniffed as the preacher glared at her until she echoed his words: "With this ring I thee wed."

Finally, they were pronounced man and wife. Together they turned and faced their friends and smiled at one another.

"We are married, Ellie. I thought this day would never come."

She peered up at him, his startlingly handsome face sending a fresh wave of exhilaration through her stomach. "But it has come, and I shall cherish this day, and you, for always." *That feeling.* No longer did she fear harsh kisses and coarse talk. Nathaniel's very presence set her heart at rest.

"We shall start our lives together as we should have done years ago." Nathaniel kicked the ground. "I'm sorry my folly stalled us for so long, dear Ellie."

Ellie's lips trembled. "I should have waited forever once I saw you return from California, even if it meant I might be a spinster. I knew then my heart could never truly belong to another."

"How could we have known what God would use for good?

My father has restored me to half of the inheritance as before I left. With Andrew in jail, I daresay we'll have to live at Woodacre for a time. And we shall have Rosamond as well, thanks to your father's change of heart." Nathaniel shook his head. "I am truly a prodigal son, and I have our Lord to thank for it. I shall spend my days preaching on His infinite grace."

Eleanor smiled. "And I shall be at your side, Nathaniel. Whatever life brings us, wherever we might dwell."

"Do you trust me, Ellie? Do you trust God to lead us?"

She felt her head nod up and down. "I do."

Nathaniel drove Eleanor to Woodacre in an elegant, open black carriage strewn with yellow roses and white silk ribbons. As the carriage turned up the drive, she caught her first glimpse of the mighty house where she would be mistress.

"Oh, Nathaniel, I don't know if I'm ready for this." She drew in a deep breath. "Woodacre is so massive, and it's been such a long time since a woman saw to it properly. I don't know if I'm the one—"

He silenced her with a kiss. "You are the only one, my sweet. God ordained you personally. He's returned us to one another for life. I love you, Ellie Pemberton." He caressed her face in his strong hands. "Welcome home, my love."

A Letter To Our Readers

Dear Reader:

In order that we might better contribute to your reading enjoyment, we would appreciate your taking a few minutes to respond to the following questions. We welcome your comments and read each form and letter we receive. When completed, please return to the following:

Rebecca Germany, Fiction Editor
Heartsong Presents
PO Box 719
Uhrichsville, Ohio 44683

Did you enjoy reading *The Prodigal's Welcome* by Kristin Billerbeck?

❏ Very much! I would like to see more books
by this author!

❏ Moderately. I would have enjoyed it more if

_____

_____

Are you a member of **Heartsong Presents**? Yes ❏ No ❏
If no, where did you purchase this book?_____

_____

How would you rate, on a scale from 1 (poor) to 5 (superior), the cover design?_____

On a scale from 1 (poor) to 10 (superior), please rate the following elements.

_____ Heroine   _____ Plot

_____ Hero   _____ Inspirational theme

_____ Setting   _____ Secondary characters

5. These characters were special because _____

_____

_____

6. How has this book inspired your life? _____

_____

_____

7. What settings would you like to see covered in future
   Heartsong Presents books? _____

_____

_____

8. What are some inspirational themes you would like to see
   treated in future books? _____

_____

_____

9. Would you be interested in reading other **Heartsong
   Presents** titles?   Yes ☐   No ☐

10. Please check your age range:
    ☐ Under 18   ☐ 18-24   ☐ 25-34
    ☐ 35-45   ☐ 46-55   ☐ Over 55

Name _____

Occupation _____

Address _____

City _____ State _____ Zip _____

Email _____

NEW MEXICO *Sunrise*

Join the Lucas, Monroe, and Dawson families as they take their claim to the "Land of Enchantment." Their struggles and triumphs blend into the sandtone mesas and sweeping sage plains of New Mexico, and their tracks are still visible along the deeply rutted Santa Fe Trail and the chiseled railways they traveled. Award-winning author Tracie Peterson brings their stories to life.

NEW MEXICO *Sunset*

*T*he saga of the Lucas, Monroe, and Dawson families, introduced in *New Mexico Sunrise*, echoes across the vast open landscape of a state in its infancy. Now the next generation must take up the pioneer spirit of their parents and lay claim to their place in a changing world.

paperback, 464 pages, 5 ³⁄₁₆" x 8"

♥ ♥ ♥ ♥ ♥ ♥ ♥ ♥ ♥ ♥ ♥ ♥ ♥ ♥ ♥ ♥

Please send me ____ copies of *New Mexico Sunrise* and ____ copies of *New Mexico Sunset*. I am enclosing $5.97 for each. (Please add $2.00 to cover postage and handling per order. OH add 6% tax.)

Send check or money order, no cash or C.O.D.s please.

Name_____

Address_____

City, State, Zip_____

To place a credit card order, call 1-800-847-8270.
Send to: Heartsong Presents Reader Service, PO Box 721, Uhrichsville, OH 44683

♥ ♥ ♥ ♥ ♥ ♥ ♥ ♥ ♥ ♥ ♥ ♥ ♥ ♥ ♥ ♥

····Heartsong····

HEARTSONG PRESENTS TITLES AVAILABLE NOW:

(If ordering from this page, please remember to include it with the order form.)